Eugene McCarthy

A Tale of Lake St. John

Comprising a Bit of History, a Quantity of Facts and a Plenitude of Fish

Stories. Second Edition

Eugene McCarthy

A Tale of Lake St. John
Comprising a Bit of History, a Quantity of Facts and a Plenitude of Fish Stories.
Second Edition

ISBN/EAN: 9783337137373

Printed in Europe, USA, Canada, Australia, Japan

Cover: Foto ©Andreas Hilbeck / pixelio.de

More available books at **www.hansebooks.com**

The Ladies seek the Ouananiche as well.

A TALE

OF

LAKE ST. JOHN

COMPRISING

A BIT OF HISTORY

A QUANTITY OF FACTS

AND

A PLENITUDE OF FISH STORIES

BY

EUGENE McCARTHY

Author of " The Leaping Ouananiche,"
" Familiar Fish," etc.

SECOND EDITION
TWENTIETH THOUSAND

MONTREAL
DESBARATS & CO.
ENGRAVERS, PRINTERS AND PUBLISHERS
1903

To those whom Fortune has presented, from her store of gifts, the particular one most dear to lovers of the rod and gun, the desire to seek the haunts of fish and game, I dedicate this work. He who casts the fly, or he who prefers the gun, can find equally satisfying sport in the territory described. The true sportsman is Nature's nobleman, and in Nature's domain, undefiled by the advance of civilization, will find all the sport that desire can picture and experience can realize.

To H. J. Beemer, Esq., who, through the expenditure of much time and money, has thrown open an hundred thousand or more square miles of virgin territory to those who love the sports and seclusion of the wilderness, I especially dedicate this.

I doubt not but that those who have in the past visited this grand country reserved for sportsmen, and those who in the future may do so, will gratefully join in this especial dedication with me.

E. McC.

INDEX.

CHAPTER   I—En route 7

"   II—The Hotel Roberval 10

"   III—The Grande Décharge 13

"   IV—Lac de Belle Rivière 21

"   V—Lake Tschotagama and the Peribonca River . . 26

"   VI—The Ouiatchouaniche and La Croche Rivers . . 26

"   VII—The Ashuapmouchouan, Lac-à-Jim, and Fifth
         Falls, Mistassini River 33

"   VIII—The Metabetchouan 39

"   IX—Other Trips to be Taken 43

"   X—The Hatchery 47

"   XI—The Saguenay 52

"   XII—Equipment Necessary 58

"   XIII—General Information 64

"   XIV—The Pro and Con. of Success and Satisfaction
         to be Found 71

INTRODUCTION.

To the sportsman, the winter reminiscences of his journeyings in quest of fishing and hunting, during the preceding season or seasons, affords, next to the trip itself, the greatest amount of pleasure. When the cold is strong without and the fire cheerful within, then do the reminiscences come to mind in full force. If alone, the thinker passes many an hour in dreamland, living over his successes and non-successes, realistic to such a degree that he can almost feel the line tighten on the fish, or see the game fall before his gun. If with his friends, stories of the past are exchanged, and many a glass is drained to the memories of former trips, and still more to the success of those to be taken in the coming year.

Spring and summer seem a long distance off. Impatience is strong within the sportsman. Will the time to seek the woods ever arrive? But one prescription can be prescribed, and that unfortunately is but a temporary relief, not a cure. After reminiscences have been exchanged, time and time again, until nothing new can be said, after the dreamer has dreamed all of the past, then does impatience become rampant and the longing for spring to come unbearable. The one semi-cure may now be applied. Primarily it consists in planning new resorts to seek, as perchance the old ones are now fished and hunted out. This is more readily accomplished by reading the varied stories of other sportsmen, as published, selecting from their experiences where to make a trip or trips. Then, between reading, selecting and planning, the time passes—the where, when and how has been decided upon—the cure has been productive of beneficial results to a greater or lesser degree.

There can be no question but that very many sportsmen are constantly seeking new territory where satisfying sport may be had. With this idea in mind, I have prepared this series of articles, descriptive of many trips that I have taken about Lake St. John, the one home of the greatest of fresh-water fish—the ouananiche. An unlimited territory is here found, with unlimited forest, plentifully stocked with game, and unlimited waters teeming with fish. Here everything is unlimited — the territory, the grandeur of scenery, the game, and the fish. Thousands of square miles, unknown, await the intrepid sportsman, who, with time at his command, can reach virgin forests and waters, where, being first to cast the fly or seek for game, secures success that he never dared dream of before. To those with limited time, the nearby trips afford, at the proper season, satisfying sport. That this is not fiction but fact, I trust that the reminiscences following will fully prove.

CHAPTER I.

"The Irishman's description of a wilderness, as being a place where the hand of a man had never set foot, properly describes the primeval wilderness we have been passing through on our railroad journey to-day."

This was the remark of a companion of mine who was making his first trip over the Quebec & Lake St. John Railway. It was aptly expressive, as the road, for two-thirds of its length, traverses a mountainous wilderness, grand in the extreme and showing but little of the advance of civilization. We had left behind the magnificent view of Quebec and the St. Lawrence valley, as the train slowly ascended the mountains, had passed successfully the surging falls of the Jacques Cartier River beneath the railroad bridge, beautiful Lake St. Joseph, and the thriving little town of St. Raymond.

Now the forest is primeval, with but little sign of the lumberman's desecration. Up and up slowly climbs the train, and from our station on the rear platform we can see the heavy grades and continuous sharp curves. An occasional small clearing, with a few log-houses, sheltering perchance railroad hands or two or three straggling settlers, forms the only break or evidence of habitation.

Some seventy miles from Quebec has been covered, and now occurs an episode—a fish story. Certainly every five minutes or less we had crossed a river or stream or passed a lake. Knowing that all of these waters were full of trout, my companion's anxiety to fish had become so strong he could scarcely restrain himself from pulling the cord to stop the train and cast his flies. We had reached the Batiscan River, whose broad, constant tumbling waters the road follows for many miles, when suddenly the train stopped. Investigation showed a cylinder-head blown out of the engine, and an hour or two delay imminent. The wires must be tapped and another engine ordered on from Quebec. Not over ten feet distant from the river, and about eight feet above it, stood the train. The black waters tumbling over the rocks formed an ideal place for trout.

"Now is your opportunity," I advised my companion. "Set up your rod and put on a cast, and satisfy your fishing fever." In a few moments, acting upon my advice, he emerged from the car, rod in hand, eager for sport.

"Why not make a new record in trout fishing?" I asked. "Stand on the steps of the car and catch your fish." Bert, as I should have named my companion, and who, by the way, is a fine fly caster, again accepted my advice, and from the lower step whipped the foamy water. A few casts and eight-inch trout is reeled in, followed by another and another. A harder strike and fight and a lusty one-pound trout is added to those on the platform. In short order nineteen trout were taken, and Bert's fever was allayed. Others tried their hand with equal success. Improperly, I have stated that this was a fish story. It is pure fact, not fiction.

The engine arrives, and again we proceed. I point out to Bert a number of club stations and club houses. Much of the territory along the road is now taken up by fish and game clubs, and grand, indeed, is the sport the members secure. Not only are trout plentiful on all sides, but moose and caribou abound as well.

With appetites sharpened by the delay, we finally reached Lake Edward, one hundred and thirteen miles from Quebec, where a stop of twenty minutes is made for dinner at a small hotel located on the lake. A few log-houses are about—all else wilderness. Again we set off, and another succession of rivers, streams and lakes is encountered. One little creek that we crossed, not over six feet wide, I call particular attention to. In the spring of 1897, I know that two fishermen took along this water, in less than one week, over four hundred and fifty pounds of trout, that they sold in the Quebec markets. This, perhaps, is one of the best indications of the fishing to be had in this country. Bert asks: "Have you fished all of these?" To which I reply: "I have not, and never expect to, as an ordinary lifetime would not afford sufficient time." Just then passing Lake Bouchette, a large body of water lying far below, I can relate that, about three years pre-

vious, a companion and myself secured two hundred and sixty-seven trout on the river flowing from the lake, at " Petite Roche " springhole, in about six hours. This seems incredible to Bert, and he says so. I reply : "One in reality cannot lie about the sport they have had in this country. If one exaggerates a little in number and size, the next catch taken from the same place and shown by others will often eclipse the fish story catch in fact."

The scenery now becomes more mountainous and rocky, the forest gives way to scrubby brush. Suddenly the train makes a sharp curve, rolling out from amongst the rocks upon a cliff. Far below, and as far as the eye can see, magnificent Lake St. John bursts into view. Bert is overcome, but finally manages to say : " No one can blame the ouananiche for taking up its home here, and I do not wonder that they are never found elsewhere."

Fifteen miles distant is the ancient village of Roberval. Nearly midway we cross the Ouiatchouan River, and back amongst the hills can plainly be seen the beautiful falls bearing that name. As the lake is in full view, it forms a pretty picture, attracting attention, and almost before one is aware the village is reached. After a short stop the train proceeds a mile beyond, to the foot of the lawn at the Hotel Roberval. Two hundred miles have been traversed through the Laurentian wilderness, and the traveller views with surprise the magnificent hotel that hospitably awaits him. While beyond expectation, the reality in comfort found exceeds even what surface indications seem to promise.

CHAPTER II.

THE HOTEL ROBERVAL.

Bert wonders constantly as each new feature of the splendid Hotel Roberval is seen. Everyone wonders in like manner. It represents an immense investment, and every detail is in perfect keeping. A more comfortable hostelry cannot be found in Canada, and, with the variety of sport to be had, it makes an ideal resort for sportsmen. Naturally Bert asks what sport can be had in the vicinity of Lake St. John, other than ouananiche fishing. In advising him what could be done and where, I spent many hours, both at the hotel and in camp, and then could not cover the subject.

Bert suggests, eagerly: "Suppose that we get up early and catch some fish before breakfast?" "Unfortunately," I reply, "you have the same erroneous idea as is held by the majority of sportsmen on their first visit to Roberval. There is no fishing from the hotel porch, or in the immediate vicinity of the hotel, except trolling in the lake, which can be done at all times, when pickerel (*brochet*), wall-eyed pike (*doré*), and some ouananiche are taken on the spoon. From the Roberval, for trout fishing, trips of from one day to any number of weeks must be had. Successful and satisfying jaunts can be arranged to fit the time at one's command."

"But how about the ouananiche fishing?" is the next query.

"At all times there is good ouananiche fishing at the Grande Décharge, in the immediate vicinity of the Island House, which is conducted by the Roberval Hotel people. It is reached by steamer in two hours across the lake."

"Is that the best and only nearby place for this fishing?" Bert asks, dubiously.

In reply, I hasten to state: "There are eighteen rivers, large and small, flowing into Lake St. John, nearly all of which furnish fine fishing at some time during the season. For two hundred to three hundred miles north, up the three great rivers—the Peribonca, Mistassini and Ashuapmouchonan—there are innumerable branches, draining hundreds and thousands of lakes, nearly all of which afford fine ouananiche fishing, and are full of trout, pickerel, pike and lake trout as well. To reach these, short or long trips may be taken. As you look across the lake to the north, there is not a settlement, except the Trappist monastery on the Mistassini, and but very few habitations to be found until Hudson Bay is reached—some five hundred miles away. You are in a cleared settlement, yet in the midst of a wilderness, surrounded by the finest fishing to be had. A few miles in any direction leaves civilization behind and you are deep in the woods."

Early the following morning Bert aroused me, stating he wanted to see and learn something regarding the surroundings, that, with our late arrival the evening previous, darkness had prevented. The early sun shone brightly on the great body of water stretched out before us, and a most magnificent sight it was. Lake St. John, thirty to thirty-five miles in diameter, is an immense inland sea, and only in a few instances can the opposite shore be discerned.

"What is there, other than the sport to be had, to interest one here?" Bert queries, after a time.

"A short question calling for a long reply," I answer; "a subject worthy of a lecture. I will tell you briefly. The village of Roberval, which, with the neighboring settlers, claims two thousand five hundred inhabitants, is well worth seeing; the quaint houses and strange *habitants*—French Canadian, Indian, and mixed. Historically the town is practically as old as Quebec. Next in order is the Montagnais Indian reservation at Pointe Bleue, four miles distant. Here is located the Hudson Bay post, and grouped around it, from June to August, are the tents of the Indians. At the post they barter their furs, and then again journey, often hundreds of miles, to hunt and trap during the long winter. Canadian history claims the Montagnais to have been the most powerful tribe of Indians on the continent. To-day, decimated by starvation and disease, but a small remnant remains. They are interesting to visit. Of special interest are their customs, manner of living, and birch-bark canoe-building. The valuable furs at the post can also be seen."

"I must see all this. What next?" Bert interrupts.

"Next in point of interest are the Ouiatchouan Falls, six miles away. They are on the river of the same name, which is the outlet of Lake Bouchette, that we passed on the cars yesterday. They are two hundred and sixty-five feet high. A large body of water passes over, and, coming through a cleft in the mountain, they form one of the grandest falls I have ever seen. Five miles from the hotel, *en route* to the falls, Mr. Beemer, the owner of the Hotel Roberval and lessee of the St. John territory, has just completed a fish-hatchery, to increase the ouananiche and trout supply, as also to raise salmon (*salmo salar*) for his waters. As this is of especial interest, we will visit it later, before we return home. Strange as it may seem, quite good roads can be found, and several most beautiful drives can be made. The scenery changes from clearing to forest, and from mountain to plain. At the hotel music, billiards, bowling, tennis and other amusements can entertain the stay-at-homes."

"How about trips on the lake? Where can one go by steamer?"

"The largest boat you see at the dock—the "Mistassini"— makes a trip to the Island House, at the Grande Décharge, every day, going over in the morning and returning at night. The other steamer you see—the "Peribonca"—runs to the Peribonca River two or three times a week. Still another boat—the "Colon"— runs up the Mistassini River to the Trappist monastery, near the first falls, which is especially worthy of a visit. Then, there is the little steamer "Undine," that can be chartered by fishing or pleasure parties at any time. I must not overlook mentioning the large mill you see over there on the shore of the lake. It is considered one of the largest in Canada, and very interesting to visit. Its principal business is sawing "deals" for shipment to England. You can now see, Bert, how much of interest there is, aside from fishing."

"I am too anxious to catch ouananiche to go sight-seeing now, but when we finish with fishing I want to see some of the things you have mentioned. Let us have breakfast, and get ready for our trip to the Grande Décharge."

CHAPTER III.

THE GRANDE DÉCHARGE.

It was a beautiful trip across the lake to the Grande Décharge, and the changing view of the rolling, forest-covered mountains magnificent. Bert, however, all anxiety to catch his first ouananiche, was busy with rods and tackle, and could only be induced to occasionally glance up. " Where will we fish ; where will we go ; and what will we see at the Décharge?" Berts asks ; and I while away the two-hour trip answering his questions.

We will each take a canoe and two guides ; first, on account of safety, and, secondly, because two cannot successfully cast for and play ouananiche in the same boat. A birch-bark canoe is absolutely the only safe craft to use in the wild waters and rapids of the Décharge, strange as it may seem. Its strength is in its very lightness and apparent weakness. That it is a most buoyant boat is its first claim, and the spring of the ribs and toughness of the bark the other. If a rock is struck with much force, it bounds off uninjured, unless a sharp point makes a small hole, in which case a few chips burning melt the gum in a cup always carried, and, with a piece of cloth, repairs are made at once. It would be impossible for one guide to manage a canoe in the rapids, and two guides and two passengers would overload for rough water. The Grande Décharge and the Petite Décharge, three miles away, form the outlets of Lake St. John. Joining ten miles below the lake, they carry away the inflowing waters of eighteen large and small rivers that feed the lake. In a journey of over forty miles to tide water at Chicoutimi the fall is about three hundred feet, which accounts for the terrific and practically continuous rapids throughout almost the entire distance. At Chicoutimi the Décharge becomes the dark, gloomy river of mystery—the Saguenay. Alma Island separates the two Décharges. Numberless islands dot the lake about the outlet, and a large number are found all along the

Grande Décharge for a dozen miles or more. Some of the rapids
can be run in a canoe, but the greater majority cannot. Those
passable are rarely, if ever, run in extreme high water. The
ouananiche fishing commences amongst the islands in the lake,
and is considered good for about twenty miles down the Décharge.
In the more quiet pools and bays, in the rough waters of the
rapids, in the foam-covered pools below, almost anywhere, the
fish is taken. The pools are numberless, and all are good. About
the islands in the lake fly casting is often successful, but there
usually, as well as down to the first rapid, trolling with flies, or a
spoon or small spinner, succeeds best. All other pools and rapids
are fished with flies. It is useless to attempt to describe the
rapids, the fishing or the scenery—it is impossible, as you will see,
Bert. I want you to see as much as our limited time will permit—
get plenty of fishing, run rapids and see the wildest flow of water
to be seen anywhere. We will stop at the Island House, and make
day trips from there. In this way we will be more comfortable
and can accomplish more."

We had been rapidly approaching the Décharge, and as I
finished, the Island House came into view about a mile distant.
Already the steamer began to feel the force of the outflowing
current of the lake, and the speed increased. In a few moments,
with steam reduced, we fairly rushed by several islands, and with a
graceful curve swung alongside the dock in front of the hotel.

Bert was the first to land, and waited impatiently for me.
"Let us secure our guides at once, and start out fishing; I am all
ready." My advice that dinner first was a necessity, and that
then we could start out for the afternoon, finally prevailed. Bert,
however, wanted to fish from the dock until dinner time. As this
did not promise success, I managed to have him give up the idea.
I found that Johnny Morel and Ferdinand La Roche, with two
other guides, had been apportioned to us, which pleased me particularly, as I had had them before, and considered them especially
valuable men.

Immediately after dinner we had a talk with the guides, and
as a result concluded to fish the pools at the foot of the Grande
Chute, some three miles down the Décharge. Embarking in our

The Ouananiche.—A 7½-lb. Specimen.

canoes, the swift current quickly carried us over the intervening
mile to the head of the first rapid below the hotel. Except in very
high water, or unless passengers are timid, this rapid is always run
with the canoes.

"You don't mean to say we are going through there?" Bert
asked, as he saw the rough water and high, leaping waves below.

"Certainly; and you will want to run all the other rapids
afterwards," I replied. I could see Bert nervously clutch the
gunwales, as his canoe rushed into the terrific current. In a
moment he had descended the first sharp incline—a slant of three
or four feet—then mounted the great wave below—tossed here and
pitched there, skilfully guided by the men between dangerous
rocks and immense waves—first up on the crest, then down almost
out of sight in the hollow—then a channel that must be avoided
and another taken. The guides calmly give a strong stroke or
two with the paddles, and the canoe glides across the leaping
waves easily and into the other course. More pitching and toss-
ing, more rocks, some fairly grazed by the canoe—ahead a continuation of the rapids absolutely impassable. Suddenly the canoe
is impelled on a slant across the wild waters, a final toss by the
waves, and it glides into a small bay, calm and smooth as a pond.
Watching Bert's passage through the rapid ahead of me, I had scarcely realized my own trip, until I was swung alongside of him, the
run safely made. We had covered in two or three minutes a distance
that required ten minutes to walk on the portage when returning.

Bert immediately exclaimed: "Let us go back and go through
again. It is the finest sport I have ever had."

"But, how about the fishing?"

"Oh! that can wait." Assuring him that he would have
many more opportunities to run rapids, he was finally content to
continue the trip. With smooth water for a distance, and two
portages, we were soon at the foot of the "Grande Chute," and,
climbing along the rocks, were at the rough waters where the
ouananiche lie. Purposely I worked slowly, stringing up my rod,
as I wanted my companion to catch the first fish, and see what he
would do with it. But a few minutes elapsed before I heard Bert
cry out: "Gee-whizz, Mac; look at that!"

He had hooked a ouananiche, and it had given its first leap. In a great majority of cases this fish takes the fly under water and foam, so that the strike is not often seen, the pull, run out of the line or a jump being the first intimation that a fish is hooked. It had so happened now. Bert had felt his line pull, immediately followed by a wild leap of the fish from the water. It was great sport to see that fish rush about, leap, and then plunge down deep. His fighting strength, aided by the rough waters, gave Bert a hard struggle, so much so that he did not speak again until his fish was brought to net. The fish weighed three and a half pounds, had jumped seven times from the water, and gave Bert thirteen minutes tussle to conquer.

"Well, what do you think of the ouananiche now?" I asked.

"I did not believe you when you said they were the hardest fighting fresh-water fish, and especially that they could teach a black bass how to fight. Now, however, I am a believer. This is the finest fishing I have ever had, and this one fish I have just killed, if I get no more, would repay me for the trip."

"Just notice, Bert, the peacock-blue shading it has. It will soon disappear, and then you will see the silver white and black of the salmon. To my mind, the ouananiche has many more and heavier black crosses and spots than the salmon, especially on the gill covers. There can be no question but that it is a descendant of the salt-water salmon, that it has run up from the sea in the past, and has continued to remain in fresh water. The new environments have depreciated it in size only, have increased the proportionate size of tail and fins—mainly, I believe, from its constant struggle with swift waters. The color and markings have changed slightly from its progenitor, and, pound for pound, it will outfight it. The flesh is salmon-pink, with the flaky texture of the salmon, more tender, and lacking in the excess of oil and fat that a fresh-run salmon has. This would naturally follow from the difference of food."

"From my knowledge of fish and fishing, I believe you are correct," Bert answered, as he finished a critical examination of the fish. "Here goes for another."

Nine fish were brought to our nets, in two and a half hours, that afternoon, and three were lost besides. The weight was from two and a half to four pounds.

Our time at the Décharge being limited, I suggested to Bert that we try a variety of fishing the following day, especially as he had had a good introduction to ouananiche fishing in rough water. We left our comfortable beds at the Island House quite early, and proceeded up the eastern shore of the lake *en route* to the Pipe River, about five miles distant, with trolling rods and lines and number five spoons. We trolled the whole distance. We took several doré, one weighing eight pounds. Arrived at the Pipe, we spent some time trolling about its mouth, determined to secure some of the large brochet, often taken there. We found an old Indian on a sloping rock on the shore, casting out a spoon fastened to an old line and pole. Suddenly he secured a strike, and the sequence was very amusing. The fish was evidently a large one, and, owing to the insecure footing the slanting rock afforded and the age and weakness of the Indian combined, the contest for superiority favored first one side and then the other. At times the old fisherman was drawn down the rock into the water, nearly to his waist; then he would in turn draw the fish almost out. We watched the struggle at close range, to render assistance if necessary. Finally the fish became tired, and the Indian, placing the pole over his shoulder, turned his back to the brochet, and proceeded, inch by inch, up the rock, dragging it, slowly and laboriously, after him. It was a very large fish, which we estimated to weigh fully thirty pounds. We secured several of these fish afterwards, but nothing heavier than sixteen pounds. Shortly after noon we returned to the Island House, and decided to troll with flies and small spinners attached to our fly rods, amongst the islands in the lake. This method only of fishing in this particular place seems to be successful at almost all times; nor was our luck that day any exception.

"The fishing we have had to-day is too tame; I want to go where we can run rapids and fish in rough water," was Bert's remark when we returned to the hotel. "Very well," I replied; "we will go down the Décharge to-morrow as far as Isle Maligne,

and camp there overnight. This will give you a surfeit of shooting
rapids, with much danger added, and plenty of good fishing."
Having made all arrangements after supper, we were able to get a
6 A. M. start. We repeated our journey of the first afternoon, and
fished many of the pools below the Grande Chute. Wherever we
saw a patch of heavy foam (*brou*), there we cast our flies, and met
with splendid success. It is not well always to give the number of
fish caught, as one's memory is liable to be defective, and a charge
of exaggeration follows guess work.

Not to spend much time at any one spot, we started down the
river, as I was anxious to try the numberless pools on our route,
many of which are never fished. The distance to Maligne from
the Island House is seven or eight miles, with practically the
whole distance a continuous mass of rapids and rough, swift
water, filled with rocks and a countless number of small islands.
In reality the places where one can take ouananiche along this
part of the river are innumerable ; at almost any rapid or eddy
some success can be had. One with ample leisure could spend
much time here and fish new pools constantly. Bert and I often
cast our flies and stopped a few moments at each specially pro-
mising place. We were very well rewarded, but not by extra large
fish. At noon we reached Cedar Rapids, and the first real attack of
nervousness was felt as the canoes rushed ahead, as though to
plunge over quite a respectable fall. This run close to danger is
necessary to reach the head of the portage. I think Bert relished it.

"You are a brave rapid runner," I said to him ; "but eat a
good lunch now, as you will need strength, fortitude, and even
'Dutch courage' to make the head of Isle Maligne." Not to be
deterred, he hurried us all at our hastily prepared meal in order to
have the "circus," as he termed it. Soon the very loud roar of
the rapids and falls about the island could be heard, and as we
approached nearer I could not but notice that the guides ceased
their conversation, sort of girded up their loins, and plainly showed
an anxious look on their faces. A piece of work both difficult and
dangerous was ahead. The head of the island divides the river,
and upon each side, beginning above it, are to me the most terrible
rapids on the Décharge. I have seen logs passing through fairly

riven into match-wood. Between the rapids is a lane of fairly
smooth water forty or fifty feet wide. To avoid the rapids and
run through the lane would be comparatively easy, were that the
only danger. Just before entering you will hear the guides say
" *Remous*," and indeed there is a whirlpool to be avoided. It is
located in the lane, and the canoes must pass between it and the
rapids—a very limited space. When the whirlpool is forming and
growing deeper, nothing could live in it. As it fills up level with
the surface of the water, then is the time to pass. The guides
have been holding the canoes and watching. Suddenly a hurried
word from the bow man, and both paddle fiercely. We fairly fly
past the danger, and in a moment we are beached on the island.

"That is all the rapid running I want to-day," was Bert's only
comment for some time.

Maligne is an island something over two miles long, and from
one-half to three-quarters of a mile wide. It is very rocky, rough,
and the lower end is a large mountain that must be crossed.
Fishing must be done from the rocks, and is good all around the
shores, although the best fishing is to be had, and the largest fish
taken, near the foot of the heavier falls. One could spend a week
here, and not begin to cover all possible and likely spots. We had
ample time to fish, and had splendid success, before the tents were
up and supper served. The fish were of good size, Bert taking one
of four pounds. The tramp over the rocks, the fishing and supper
dispelled Bert's nervousness—and mine.

"Are there any more impassable places where they are foolish
enough to run a canoe, like that at the head of the island?" Bert
asks through the smoke of his pipe. "There are other wicked
places, and a number, too, below. Don't you want to go around
and come down to the island again to-morrow? You always want
to run a rapid a second time."

"Principally not. I don't object to a rapid, but I do object to
skimming along the brink of miniature Niagaras."

"About a mile below us, just where the Petite Décharge flows
in, is the Vache Caille rapids, that are very wicked, and a mile or
two below the Gervais. They are treacherous, indeed ; but it is
sport to run the possible places. We will not have time to make

them." Bert had rolled up in his blanket, and I heard a sleepy voice say, "Thank heaven!"

The next morning we crossed the mountain, after breaking camp, and on the summit, some five hundred or six hundred feet high, we had a most magnificent view. The grandeur of the long stretches of tumbling rapids made a panorama unsurpassed. At the foot of the island we fished a number of pools, with the same good success. It is an exciting trip across the rapids from Maligne to Alma Island, and looks impassable. Our only mishap was to ship a little water. We portaged to a point above the Maligne Rapids, and then took our canoes to ascend the river. As it takes practically all day to make the return journey, we did not stop to fish. Again reaching the Island House, Bert suggested that our limited time for the Décharge was about up; so we concluded to leave on the steamer next day. I fear the passage to Maligne had destroyed his taste for canoeing through rapids.

In fishing the pools near the hotel, the following morning, before leaving, Bert had an experience I will relate in his own words.

"In casting in a pool—I was using two flies—I had a double strike and succeeded in hooking both fish. The one that took the dropper must have been a strong fish, as, after a few struggles and jumps, he departed, having broken the fly. The other, a much smaller fish, I continued playing, and had him about tired out, when I got a terrific strike that nearly doubled up the rod and myself as well. I could not imagine what it was any more than can you now. The strain on the rod was very great, but not much fighting—more of a dead weight. I finally got the fish to the canoe, and as Johnnie started to net it he exclaimed, "Two fish!" Sure enough it was. The ouananiche was a small one, perhaps one and a half pounds. Tightly fastened to it was a pickerel of seven or eight pounds, with fully half the ouananiche down its throat. It had gripped its prey so savagely, its mouth was completely filled, and its hooked teeth set in so deeply that it could not let go. Here is the combination in proof." It was a combination, indeed, that he held up before me, and just as he stated. "I am going to have them mounted just as they are"—and he did.

Out for Ouananiche. Island House.

CHAPTER IV.

LAC DE BELLE RIVIÈRE.

Our next trip was to Lac de Belle Rivière, and a most successful one it proved to be. The Roberval Hotel people provided guides, tents, blankets, camp equipment and provisions, in fact, all necessary for a camping trip in the woods, as they always do. This is a great advantage, as one needs to come to Lake St. John provided with only suitable clothing and tackle. Bert was very enthusiastic over the trip, and he stated he had never had any really first-class trout fishing, and had never taken one of two pounds. I had agreed that the trip would furnish both, with possibly the sight of a caribou as well.

We took the train from the hotel in the evening, reaching St. Jerome, on the Chicoutimi branch of the Quebec & Lake St. John Railway, about 9 o'clock. We sought the little inn of mine host Gauthier, and were well provided for. Before we turned in we had arranged with him for an early start. He was to provide buckboards for transportation of ourselves, guides and equipments. We also arranged to rent his log camp at the lake and his canoes as well. It is well to make a bargain for all in advance, which can usually be done at less than the original price asked.

Lac de Belle Rivière lies about fifteen miles south of Lake St. John, in the midst of the woods, and is reached over the remains of what was known as the government road, that originally extended to Quebec ; now in disuse and largely impassable, except this portion, which could well be called the same. Gauthier has made the bridges passable, and that is all. Two deep ruts, full of rocks, and mud-holes, form the road. Completely overgrown, with alders overhanging, one naturally prefers to make the last nine miles on foot. The first six miles of road after leaving St. Jerome are very good. About mid-afternoon we reached our lake, and concluded not to go up to the springholes to fish until the morrow. Just in front of the cabin the outlet leaves the lake, forming Belle Rivière, quite a respectable stream. Across it are the remains of the old government bridge and a broken dam. About the bridge and dam, I knew of old, large trout could always be found ; so, stringing up our rods and using a Parmacheene Belle and Silver Doctor for flies, Bert and I started to get a catch for supper. With four guides, three drivers and ourselves to supply, with fearful appetites engendered by the rough road, we felt we had a contract on hand. Bert took the first fish, one pound, on his second cast, and I a smaller one just after. Then the sport became fast and furious. Two fish at a time was a common occurrence. Finally Bert hooked a big one that tipped the scales at two and a half pounds, and with that we stopped fishing. We had a supply for supper and breakfast as well. We sat on the old bridge fully an hour, and watched the trout jumping. It was a beautiful sight, as the constant breaking-water of the fish had the effect of heavy raindrops steadily falling.

"This is only a preliminary to the fishing you will have on the lake," I advised Bert. "This is where you get the small fish ; to-morrow you will find large ones."

"I cannot see how you can improve on this. I have just caught more and larger trout than I ever had the good fortune to do before. I cannot imagine anything better." However, Bert had come to believe my promises in regard to fish, and was as anxious as I for the morrow and the grand fishing it would bring.

Immediately after breakfast Bert and I, with our guides, in two canoes, started up the lake, which, by the way, is seven miles long, determined to try our luck in the first or "Three-mile Springhole." At this point quite a large stream, called Rivière Sauvage, enters the lake from the west. It enters in a good-sized bay, and for several rods its channel cuts a clear course through the lily pads. In the channel the water is from six to ten feet deep, while on either side it is about four or five feet deep. The guides held the canoes, using the paddles as stakes, at the edge of the pads, moving slowly along when necessary. We started casting at once, and almost with the first cast commenced taking fish as well—large ones at that and plenty of them. The illustration accompanying shows that day's catch. Incidentally, we kept our .

Trout Pool, Outlet Lac de Belle Rivière.

surplus fish in moss, which, with other catches, were taken to Hotel Roberval on our return and served to the guests.

Bert secured a five pound and five and a quarter pound trout that day, while I was forced to be content with a four pound. I have never seen a trout under one-half pound taken from this springhole, and did not then. Here one does not get a strike every cast, nor anything like it, as large trout must be coaxed; but our all day's work aggregated some sixty fish, from one-half to five and one-quarter pounds, averaging large.

"I never believed there was any such fishing possible," Bert remarked, on our return to camp that night; "but if you say we will catch whales, and many of them, to-morrow, I will not question it.'

Again I repeat that one cannot tell "fish stories" in regard to the fishing at Lake St. John and vicinity.

The next day we concluded to fish the upper springhole or the inlet at the head of the lake, and possibly make a portage to another small lake about half a mile from the head, to catch a few trout there, and, incidentally, try and see a bear or caribou, as this little lake with an unpronounceable Indian name is noted for both.

Midway down the lake on our seven mile journey are the "Narrows," noted for being a great crossing place for caribou. Silently and with care the guides approached the spot, and suddenly Prosper, one of the guides, exclaimed, in an excited whisper: "*Caribou! caribou! deux caribous!*" and indeed there were two caribou just entering the water to cross. As the open season was nearly a month distant, we could only sit and watch them buoyantly swim the lake, and imagine what a good shot we could make at them, and how good their steaks would taste. I can almost swear that my fingers made dents in my rifle barrel, so hard did I grip it. Bert claims he bent his, but this I cannot verify.

We finally reached the springhole at the head of the lake, which, while not as large as the other and does not have as large fish, is similar in appearance, and is full of smaller trout.

This point afforded splendid sport, and we took an immense number of fish, but mostly small, one and a half pounds being the largest fish taken. As we could only use a small quantity, we took

the trout from the hooks carefully and put them back into the
water. This is a rule sportsmen invariably follow, as it still affords
the pleasure of catching the fish, without uselessly destroying
them. As we had seen caribou, and did not wish to have our
hearts broken again by seeing others, and as a heavy rain and
wind was brewing, we concluded to give up our portage to the
other lake and returned to camp.

The following morning broke fair, and, in accordance with a
plan made the previous evening, we made an early start, with our
guides and canoes, for Lac au Cèdre. Crossing the lake from the
cabin, we ascended a small inlet for some distance, and then made
a half-mile portage, coming out on a small circular lake. This we
crossed, and, following this outlet a few rods, it led us into a lake
fully a mile long, noted both for fine fishing and caribou. Without
stopping we continued the length of the lake and down its outlet
for about half a mile, which then flowed into another fine fishing
lake about three-quarters of a mile long. From this a quarter mile
portage along the outlet, all rapids, brought us to au Cèdre. This
is a beautiful L-shaped lake, fully two miles long. In the mouth
of the main inlet, and up the inlet itself, most wonderful fishing
can be had. Bert claims he could have filled a canoe there in half
a day, and I believe it possible.

Here we found many fresh caribou signs, but did not see any
of the animals themselves. A deserted beaver-dam was also found.
In the second lake, on our journey back, we saw three caribou at
some little distance, quietly feeding. We tried our flies on all the
lakes, returning, and found the fish plentiful and eager to take our
flies. We spent the four days following on Belle Rivière, fishing
the Three-mile Springhole almost entirely, although Bert went
several miles up the Sauvage River and took an immense amount
of small trout. There was no let up to the fishing at the springhole either in number or size. It seemed also that any fly was
taken. I even placed a bit of soiled cotton cloth on a plain snell
hook, and, casting that, took several fish. We returned to the
Roberval with two tent bags full of trout, as we had been requested
to bring them a good quantity. Displayed in a row on the floor,
they made a beautiful sight, and were the means of causing many

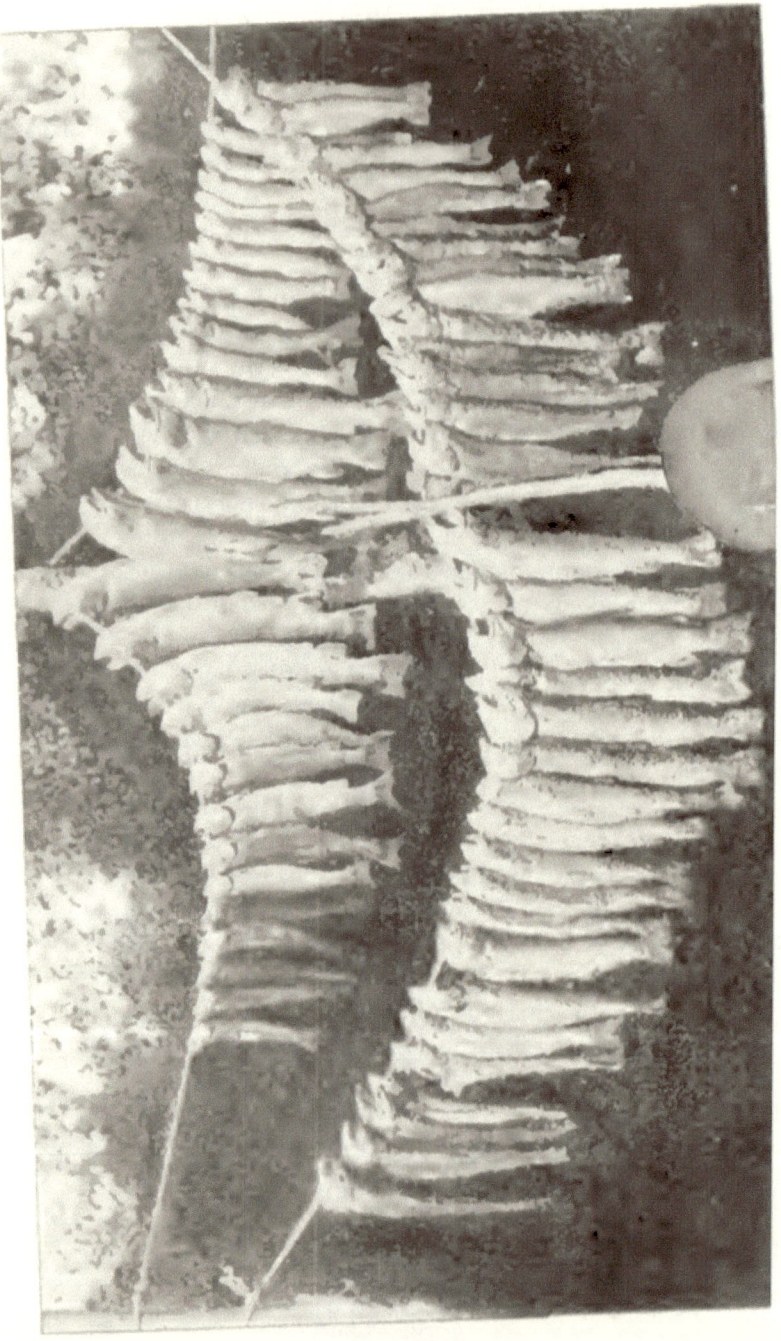

who saw them register a silent vow to seek Lac de Belle Rivière at some future time.

I neglected to state that Bert secured seven spruce partridges, going over the road coming in, while walking ahead of the waggons. I secured several black duck also on the lake.

It is well to mention that a fine trip can be made south from Belle Rivière, through two or three lakes and portages, to the Rivière aux Ecorces and into the lake of the same name. All of these waters are noted for very large trout and caribou as well. It is a trip rarely made, owing to difficulties and the considerable time necessary to make it.

CHAPTER V.

Lake Tschotagama.

There is nothing more conducive to cement friendship with one's fellow-sportsmen in the woods than the long evenings spent in tent or camp. It being after the evening meal—generally the principal one of the day—a full stomach brings peace and contentment, aided by a pipe and a snapping fire for warmth and cheer. Many are the reminiscences of previous trips retold, and each in turn recounts his personal experience. This was especially true of Bert and myself. He had related a number of trips he had made to both the Adirondacks and Maine, and had ended by saying that for variety, quality and quantity of sport, neither, in his estimation, could equal his present experience. "I am so well pleased with my first trip here," he said, "that I have determined to take my vacation in the Lake St.-John country each year hereafter. I wish you would tell me of the trips to be taken, so that I can make also." It was a pleasure to do this; and I present them as told to him.

"It was by accident that I heard of Lake St. John, and made my first trip there ten years ago. The first two trips I devoted entirely to ouananiche, at the Grande Décharge. That was before the days of the Island House, and we always stopped at a portable camp, where we lived very comfortably. In those days the ouananiche fishing was wonderful; seventy-five to one hundred fish—and large ones—could be taken in a day. I have visited Lake St. John every year since, and, commencing with the third, have always taken a different trip away from the lake each season."

"What was your first one?" Bert asks.

"My first trip was to Lake Tschotagama. I had heard much about it from the guides, and concluded to go, but could get no one to undertake the trip with me. Coming up on the train from Quebec that year I had the good fortune to meet an English sportsman—William Hayes—an assistant district attorney of London. I explained the trip I expected to make, and he was eager at once to accompany me. Lake Tschotagama lies close to the Peribonca River, emptying into it fifty or sixty miles up from Lake St. John. In consulting with the guides—the head one being Paul Savard, who was very familiar with the country—they suggested our making the trip by way of a number of rivers and lakes, and returning down the Peribonca. This we decided to do. All arrangements being made, with tents, provisions and four guides, we started early one morning from camp on a three weeks' trip.

"We descended the Décharge to just above the Cedar Rapids, where the Mistook River enters. A short portage took us around the rapids near the mouth, and we started to ascend it. We followed the river until night, camping at the mouth of a branch flowing in. The following day we ascended the branch, which quickly led us to Lake Brochet. From here we made a portage to Rivière des Aulnaies, which we followed up all day. In both rivers we found plenty of trout, but small. Leaving the river, we camped, knowing that on the morrow we had to face a hard four-mile portage to a small river, an outlet of Lac à l'Ours. Savard knew of a settler near by, and secured his horse and primitive cart to convey our canoes and baggage, which expedited matters very much, although the road through the woods was vile.

"By noon we had covered the four miles, and found the water too low in the river to make it passable for canoes. Nothing remained but to go four miles further, to the lake. This led through a *brûlé* or burned clearing. It was a fearfully warm day, and not a drop of water was found anywhere. When we reached the lake, Hayes and I, after removing only a portion of our clothing, plunged into the outlet, drinking our fill and getting cool as well. Afterwards, while sitting on a log with my feet in the water, I took a six-foot leader, with a single fly, and floating it below me, secured, almost at my feet, enough small trout for supper." (No remark from Bert.)

"From here our route led through two other small lakes and connecting rivers, from which, by a rather long portage, we reached the River Blanche, which, five miles below, enters Lake Tschotagama. The river, as is the lake, is bordered by very high mountains, very precipitous, and affording a panorama of magnificent scenery. We entered the lake, and started at once for a camping place, five miles down.

"Savard suggested trolling, but by some oversight I did not have a spoon with me. Hayes found a small pearl spoon, about No. 3 or No. 4, which he attached to his casting line. After a few moments, a shout from him caused me to have my men paddle the canoe over to him. 'I have hooked a log or whale, or something, Mac; I can't move it.'

"'*Gros brochet*,' answered Paul, sententiously. As the fish would not come to the canoe, the canoe was paddled to the fish. Paul was in the stern, and with a blow of the paddle stunned the fish. It was too large to take into the canoe, so grasping it by the eyes and gills, the other guide rapidly paddled to a sandy shore ahead. Paul was obliged to jump out into about three feet of water to save and land the fish, as it had become lively again.

"It was a brochet, and an immense one. It measured over fifty inches, and weighed forty-nine pounds when placed on the scales at Roberval, a week later. Hayes was delighted, and said : 'I will have that mounted in Quebec, and take it to England. I want to show them that fish, as well as everything else, is great in America. I never saw a fish of this kind weighing over six pounds over there.' The guides wrapped it in moss and birch-bark, and Hayes carefully lugged it over all portages on the way out. I think it was his bedfellow at night also. It was afterwards mounted by Murgatroyd, at Quebec, and exhibited there and in New York.

"We camped on a beautiful point, from which a view of the whole lake, nine miles long, could be had. After supper, being anxious to equal my companion's catch, I started out with the same spoon to try. I had been trolling but a few minutes, when I got a terrific strike. I held the fish only for a moment, when fish and spoon departed. Something had broken. There was no question but that it was a very large fish. Fortunately I found an old minnow gang in my kit, with which I used a strip of pork in lieu of a minnow. It did not seem to attract the brochet, but I did

A 25-lb. Pike. Lake Tschotagama.

succeed in taking a fourteen-pound lake trout and two ouananiche
before dark.

"The next day we tried our flies, with but poor success,
securing only three or four quite small ouananiche. Again trolling
with the gang, we secured several lake trout and some small
brochet. Just before dusk we tried flies again near the shore and
had excellent success, securing several ouananiche from three to
four pounds and a two and a half pound brook trout.

"Paul had constantly talked of the wonderful falls and rapids
of the Peribonca, so we started the following morning to make a
trip down, anxious to see them all. It is useless to attempt to
describe the eleven falls, as it would be impossible. Much of the
river seems to have hewn its course through rock. Some of the
falls are quite high, notably the first below Tschotagama, which is
certainly fifty or sixty feet. None of the rapids could be run by
our canoes entire, but occasionally portions equal to those in the
Grande Décharge gave us all the thrilling excitement we cared
for. In many of the pools at the foot of the various rapids we tried
our flies for ouananiche, and were very successful. It was my
fortune to secure one of six and a half pounds that afforded me
much sport to land. We completed our trip with a notable per-
formance on the part of our guides. We left the third falls one
morning at 4 A. M., in a hard rainstorm. Reaching Lake St. John,
it was necessary to skirt along the shore, it being too large a lake
to attempt to cross. We had supper at the mouth of the Mistassini
River; from there we paddled across to Pointe Bleue, and then to
the Roberval, which we reached about 11.30 P. M. We had covered
over forty miles, mostly through the rough waters of the lake—
a notable day's journey.

"For beautiful scenery, fine fishing and a plenitude of excitement, I consider the trip up the Peribonca unequalled. As it is
from three hundred to four hundred miles long, one need not feel
cramped for room or fear to meet too many other sportsmen. A
side trip can be made up the Little Peribonca or the River Aleck,
which lead to other rivers and lakes innumerable. All swarm with
ouananiche and trout. They are rarely, if ever, fished, so that
virgin sport can be had."

CHAPTER VI.

THE OUIATCHOUANICHE AND LA CROCHE RIVERS.

"That Peribonca trip must have been a grand one," Bert remarks. "I think I will take that next year, unless there is a better one to attract me ahead of it. By the way, are there not more trips to be taken that are not full of high falls, rough rapids, rocks and danger? As I have told you, I do not like taking constant chances in these Niagara-like places. I want to hear something about calm, peaceful waters, as it were. I admit there is magnificent mountain scenery to burn; now give me something more quiet, without the scenery."

"I fear, Bert, that your taste for wild, rough scenery and waters has been perverted since the Décharge trip. However, I will tell you of a pretty trip that can be made up the Ouiatchouaniche River."

"Omit rocks and other rough things, and I will listen quietly," Bert enjoins.

"I made this jaunt with another friend, whom I will designate as Jack, that being a short and easy name to mention. On this trip we had Patrick and Prosper Clary, Amab Gill and Malek—the first two half and the others full blood Montagnais Indians. Most excellent men they are and whom I can always recommend. Patrick is now chief of the tribe. The Ouiatchouaniche is rather a small river, but comes from a long way back in the woods. The first nine miles from the lake are a succession of small rapids. Above these canoes are taken, and one can easily ascend between thirty and forty miles. We sent on our canoes, tents and provisions on buckboards around the nine miles by road very early in the morning. We followed a little later, and upon reaching the dead water found everything in readiness to proceed.

"We reached a pretty springhole in time for dinner, and we took trout enough in a few minutes sufficient for four guides and

A Stop for Dinner on the Portage. Ouiatchouaniche River.

ourselves. I advised Jack to troll his flies behind his canoe. The result was a constant succession of strikes from small trout. The first portage is over a very steep hill, but the water being at a good height, the guides dragged the canoes up through the rapids, saving us a hard climb.

"Towards night we found the river widened out to about half a mile, and was simply full of lily pads, without any sign of a channel through them. At the head of this we camped. Out from the camp about twenty feet was a little island, on which the guides placed us. Jack got his flies working first, and the result was so wonderful, I simply stood and watched. At every cast the water seemed to boil with trout. Jack is an old trout fisherman, and his remark was : 'I wish we could photograph this, as no one would believe such fishing could be possible.'

"Near this point a portage of a mile can be made to Round Lake, noted for large trout, and plenty of them. A noted and learned judge went there a year ago, on my recommendation. On his return he reported as follows : 'You advised me to go to Round Lake for good sport trout fishing. My idea of such sport is to cast a fly with a pole and play your fish. I regret to say I had no sport. I cannot consider it such when, in taking my leaders and flies from my fly-book and arranging them, trout persist in jumping from the water and taking the flies in my hands.' This is *verbatim* his report, and, from such a source, cannot be doubted."

"Be careful, Mac," Bert interposes, "or this story will have a far from peaceful effect immediately."

"All I can say in reply, Bert, is to go and try it yourself. The next day we passed through Lake Edmund, a widening of the river, about a mile long by a half mile wide. The inlet of this is the continuation of the river, but is much smaller than below. Within a few miles we found not less than six fresh bear tracks where they had crossed, but did not see any bear. Shortly after noon we left the river and made a four-mile portage. In the midst of this we found an Indian winter camp, and upon the trees surrounding a quantity of bear and beaver skulls."

"Jack wanted one of the latter, but the Indians demurred. 'You take him, no luck.' As an explanation Patrick stated the

Indian belief to be that the spirit of every bear or beaver killed must be propitiated, else no more would be killed. To this end the heads are cleaned and placed on a tree, with a piece of tobacco put in the mouth. I have often seen the skulls, but never any signs of the tobacco. I fear Indian cupidity for this article outweighs superstitious fear.

"A short distance beyond the camp we came to what is called 'Les Jardins.' Here are hundreds of acres covered with a white species of moss about three inches high, and perfectly dry to the taste. It is the favorite food of both moose and caribou. No underbrush and but few trees grow in it, so that one can see a long distance. It was not our good fortune to see any such large game, however. We spent another day crossing several small lakes, with portages between, in all of which we had fine trout fishing. We also secured quite a number of black ducks and spruce partridges. At the end of the third day we reached the Croche River, where we spent several days fishing it and its tributaries. These waters were fairly alive with trout, and we were well repaid for our trip in consequence. The Croche River flows into the St. Maurice, which empties in turn into the St. Lawrence at Three Rivers. One could continue down to the St. Maurice and then up that river. It leads to an unknown section of country, where the possibilities for hunting and fishing are not only unlimited but impossible to appreciate. We spent two weeks on this trip, and I consider it one of the most pleasant and successful that I have ever taken. Now, I trust, Bert, this has been 'peaceful' enough for you."

"It would have been had you not spoiled it by that 'rough' fish story that you attributed to the judge."

CHAPTER VII.

THE ASHUAPMOUCHOUAN—LAC-À-JIM—FIFTH FALLS MISTASSINI RIVER.

"If you want to take a trip, Bert, that will give you all varieties of scenery, all varieties of water, and all varieties of fish, with the possibility of some good shooting added, figure on about two weeks away from the hotel. Go up the Ashuapmouchouan River, thence by a series of rivers and lakes cross over to the Mistassini, thence back to Lake St. John."

"I suppose, of course, there is to be found any quantity of those miniature Niagaras," Bert answers, "that serve to keep one's nerves on edge and hair on end?"

"Yes, indeed; any quantity. Without them, however, you would not have ouananiche pools, and, naturally, but poor fishing. Then, too, rapids add that spice to the trip that makes it especially grand and enjoyable. Of course, the element of danger is there—so there is in any journey one may undertake—no more. Your canoemen are educated to handle the birch-bark craft from infancy, and their management is perfection. They know every foot of the rapids perfectly, and when high water or aught else increases the element of danger then they will not run you through them. Rapids unknown to them they will not attempt to shoot, unless they are very easy, or, by first studying them carefully, find they can do so safely. If danger is possible from any cause they will request you to make a portage around, while alone they will make the run with the baggage. By remembering this, as well as the fact that they, too, value their lives as highly as do you, and especially noticing their expertness, one soon gains full confidence, all idea of fear disappears, and the running of rapids becomes most enjoyable."

"Perhaps you are right, Mac; but I need more experience to feel as you do. But how about that trip you just mentioned?"

"Well, Jack and I made this trip also, and spent two weeks doing it. The start is made up the Ashuapmouchouan, which can be made by canoe all the way—by chartering the "Undine," which will take you to the first falls near St. Félicien—or by driving from the hotel around the head of the lake over a good road, and then over a bad one to the head or the first falls. The latter is the favorite, as it shortens the trip materially—a day and a half at least—as some of the first portages are long and hard to make. This 'River-where-they-watch-for-the-moose' is as rough or rougher than the Peribonca. In places the current is more swift and the progress slow. There are two or three more portages around falls and a long lake-like stretch of water from the fourth falls (the Chute-à-l'Ours) to where the river is finally left. This takes a good hard day's work to cover. One must go prepared for a good big number of portages, and some hard ones, on this trip; therefore go prepared as light as possible. Jack said : 'All we did for two days after we left that river with the long name was to walk much, ride little, and jump out of the canoe for another portage just as we sat down in it." Ponds, lakes and connecting streams are plentiful but small. Lake Brochet is the largest—about two miles long—and here we camped, as we were not in a hurry and wanted to get some of the great brochet and doré the lake holds. Of course they are caught trolling, and one's spoon hardly gets out the length of the line before it is viciously taken. Jack remarked : 'We could have caught a million, but, not caring to have our spoons all demolished, we stopped at a small fraction of one per cent., practically all of which we threw back, as we could not use them.' "

"How much did that fraction amount to, and how large were they?" Bert asks, incredulously.

"My recollection is we took about twenty, and nothing above eight or ten pounds. Please, do not question my fish stories, Bert ; I am trying to keep them within the bounds of reason. I don't want to be called a 'fish prevaricator' in advance. Then next we struck a little creek so narrow that the alders on each side fairly interlaced overhead. The guides stated that there was water enough for the canoes, and that we would go down it some five or

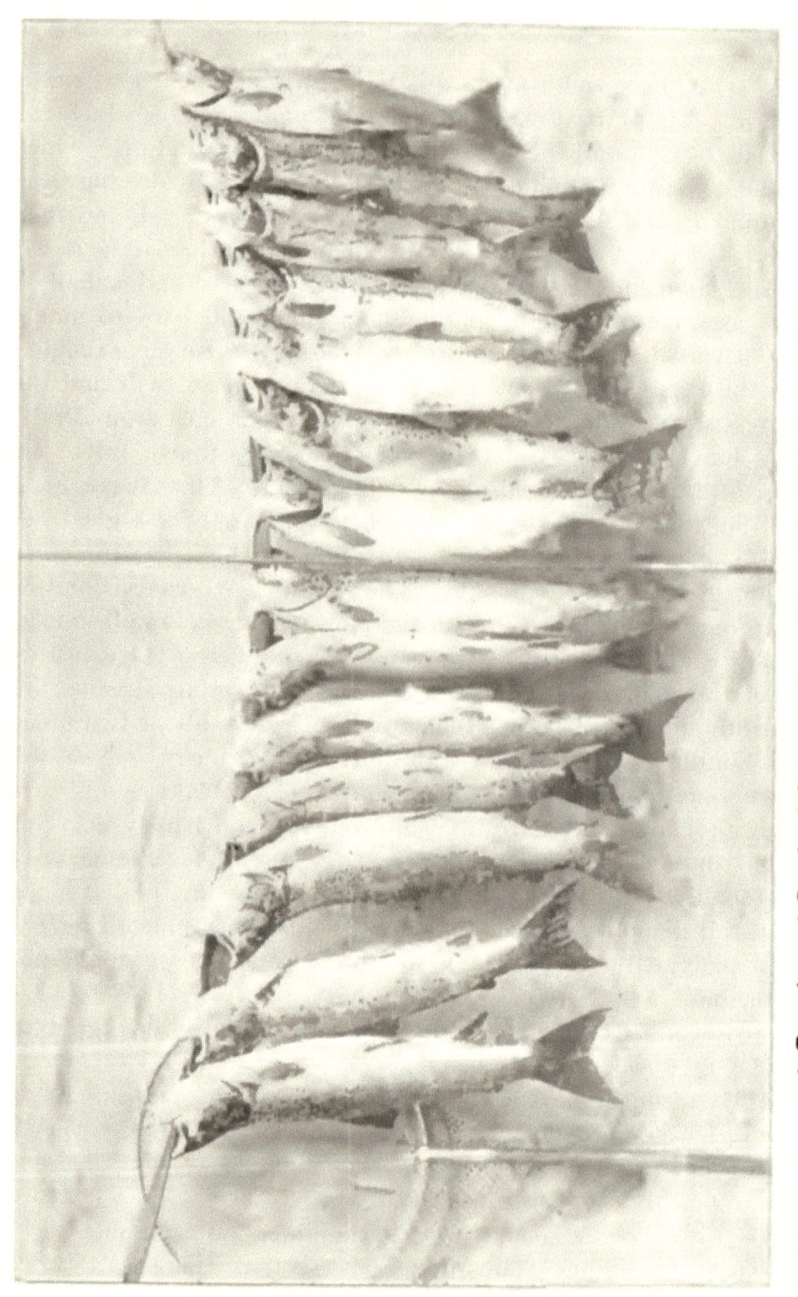

A Four-hours' Catch of Ouananiche.—Net. eighteen inches in diameter.

six miles. It was a perfect 'sheol' hole for black flies. Between fighting them and trying to preserve one's eyesight and skin from the scraping of the bushes fairly exhausted us. Jack has always claimed the branches smoothly wore off a three day's growth of beard. That part of the trip is like the road to Lac de Belle Rivière, only worse. With this and a two and a half mile portage through a burned clearing left behind, we reached Lac-à-Jim. This lake, named from an old Indian who formerly made it his hunting grounds—happy ones, I hope—is fully eight miles long, and a mighty handsome sheet of water. We remained in camp here two days, and, while we had no luck at all with our flies, we had most splendid success trolling. We took five kinds of fish—ouananiche, brochet, doré, lake trout and brook trout. Numbers and size I have forgotten now, but both were very large.

"We soon tired of the fishing, and, cutting our visit short, we started down the outlet—the Wassiemska—to the Mistassini River, into which it empties. This is a great river to run rapids in, and would not suit you, feeling as you do now. Really I believe its whole course is just one long rapid. I do not recall much, if any, smooth water. There were a number of portages, too, that delayed us. We entered the Mistassini at the tenth falls. With a rapid current and short portages around the four chutes intervening, we reached our Mecca—the fifth falls. With one exception, I have had more satisfying ouananiche fishing at that point than at any other place, and have visited it several times in consequence.

"The falls are about four hundred feet long and sheer thirty feet high. On the east is a small wooded island, and then a narrower fall, perhaps fifteen feet wide, broken into three jumps, the lower one twelve or fourteen feet clear. The large fall being impassable, the smaller one forms a natural fish-way, and it is here the fish ascend. Camp is always pitched on the island—a most delightful, cool place, and absolutely free from mosquitoes and black flies. Aside from the fishing, it is a most picturesque spot to camp on, and the distant roar of the falls is a charming additional attraction.

"I believe the most successful fishing is to be had here, beginning about the first to the middle of July and continuing well

through the month of August. In the rough water at the foot of
the main falls, about the patches of foam or *brou* in the wide bay
just below, and especially at the foot of the smaller falls, is the
best fishing to be had. Here, as well as elsewhere, the fish have
off days, but with a stay of a few days you will secure satisfying
sport. The fish average quite large and are lusty fighters, since
only large and strong fish can ascend the various falls on the river.
I counted no less than twenty-seven ouananiche ascend the lower
jump of the smaller falls in an hour. As I said, it is twelve or
fourteen feet high, and the fish would ascend in the very middle of
the falling water. Occasionally they would fail and fall back, only
to try again. The ouananiche have a hard time between being
attacked by brochet and being dashed against the rocks. I have
taken many on the rivers not only with old scars, but also with
large, gaping, fresh wounds from both causes.

"Between the second and lower jump of the small falls is
quite a deep pool in the rocks, perhaps twelve feet wide and
twenty feet long, concerning which I can relate a true fish story,
in which the other fellow figured. So many fish were jumping the
falls that day, which I noticed while fishing at the foot, I advised
Jack to try his flies in the pool, and see if he could take one there,
where they would naturally rest. He had been casting but a few
moments, when a shout indicated a fish. Anxious to see his success in such a confined space, I turned my rod over to my guide
and scrambled up the rocks to see the fun. Truly he was having a
lively time, and with a large fish, as we could see when it jumped
from the water. There was no holding him as he darted here and
there. Suddenly he went over the falls into the river below.
Jack let his reel run free, and said something strong, I fear,
although the roar of the water made it sound indistinct. There he
stood, with a blank look on his face, gripping his rod and the line
jumping here and there on the brink of the falls. I doubt if more
than one or two minutes had elapsed when his fish jumped up the
falls and again thrashed about the pool. It was about exhausted
with its high and lofty tumbling, and was soon brought to net. I
recall its weight was nearly five pounds. Jack bore his honors
meekly, and retired for an hour or two to rest his shattered nerves."

Ouananiche Pool. Fifth Falls. Mistassini River.

Pausing after this effort, Bert interposed : " Had you not better stop there for the night? I desire to sleep without a nightmare that such stories will surely bring on. The judge's story was bad enough ; but this one—phew ! what will the next one be ? "

" Just the same, Bert, this is fact, not fable," I replied ; " and it in reality happened—you have my word for that. As I have nearly finished, I will conclude and avoid any further distressing stories, to-night at least. I have always had my best fishing at the fifth falls on rainy or threatening, dark days, and in fishing from the rocks. I believe the moving about of canoes there disturbs the fish greatly.

" I neglected to state that all of the trip I have described affords splendid duck and partridge shooting, and is a great locality for bear. A number have been shot in the past few years at different points.

" With regret we left our camp about 8 A. M. one morning, and started for Roberval. The first four portages on the Mistassini are all within a distance of six miles below the fifth falls. All are short, sharp and impassable. To ascend occupies two hours or a little more—to descend, less than half that time. Between the second and third falls the River Rat flows in. The guides advise me it is the outlet of a large lake of the same name, but a long distance up, and a bad river to canoe on. I do not know of anyone ever going up there. A short distance below the first falls the Au Foin or Mistassibi River flows in. It is apparently quite a large stream, and, I am advised, furnishes good ouananiche fishing at its various falls. I do not know of any sportsmen having gone up this river either. A short distance up the austere Trappist monks have a monastery, with quite a little settlement about them. It is well worthy a visit. As it was not steamer day, we started to make the trip down the river and across the lake in our canoes—a distance of about thirty-five miles. The river to the lake—twenty miles is very swift, and as we had a good wind blowing down the river, we made wonderful speed. We tried a blanket sail that aided us materially. Such a sail is easily made, and is absolutely safe. Two poles about six feet long are placed V-shape in the bow of the canoe and held in place by the bow guide's feet. A corner of the blanket is tightly tied to the top of each pole, which spreads it to its full width. To the lower corners strings are attached, which the guide holds, one in each hand. In case of a squall or sudden hard blow, the strings are released and the feet removed from the poles and the whole thing collapses in a moment. So rapid was our progress, with paddle, current and sail aiding, that, with a short stop for lunch included, we made the twenty miles down the river in less than three hours, and then covered the fourteen or fifteen miles across the lake to Roberval, reaching there about 4 P. M.

"I can only add, Bert, if you cannot make the round trip through Lac-à-Jim, do not fail to go up to the fifth falls of the Mistassini, above all."

"All the trips you describe are so satisfactory in every way," Bert replies, "I don't know which to take first. I think I will draw lots to decide. But with a limited vacation season each year, I fear it will take a decade to made them all. What are you going to describe to-morrow night?"

"I think my favorite trip—that on the Metabetchouan River."

"Any fish stories?" Bert asks, with a yawn.

"Yes ; big ones, as far as number and size are concerned."

CHAPTER VIII.

THE METABETCHOUAN.

"The Metabetchouan River, with its length of about sixty or seventy miles, affords unlimited fishing to two large clubs—the Amabalish and Philadelphia Fish and Game Clubs, who lease the river, with the exception of the first eight or ten miles, which are controlled by Mr. Beemer for the guests of the Roberval. As soon as the ice goes out in the spring, magnificent ouananiche fishing is had in the mouth of the river where it flows into Lake St. John. From then until mid-August but few fish are taken. Following that time until the season closes, September 15th, superb fishing can be had at the first, second and third pools, located some eight miles up the river. Just above the third pool is a succession of falls, one being fully thirty feet high, which is, of course, impassable for ouananiche. The three pools are natural spawning-beds that the fish seek, and are held there from ascending further by the falls. Of late years I have always fished them just before the close of the season, and have taken more and larger fish than at any other point. Added to this that the location is in the midst of the grandest piece of mountain scenery to be found, makes it simply an ideal, perfect fishing place."

"How do you reach these pools?" Bert interrupts. "More rough canoe work? I firmly believe if the officers of the accident insurance company that I have a policy in should see some of the canoe-through-rapids trips I am taking, they would cancel it at once."

"You need not worry, Bert; this trip is perfectly harmless. It can be made in two ways. From the Metabetchouan bridge station on the railroad you can go up the river by canoe three miles to the foot of the rapids, and then portage five miles over the rocks. This is too tough a trip for me, so I prefer the other route for this and other reasons. Go to St. Jerome from Roberval, and get our friend Gauthier, who drove us to Belle Rivière, to drive this trip. Five miles of it are over the Belle Rivière road, then a turn to the right. Five miles more brings you to a turn out through the woods, finally leading to a clearing containing a very comfortable log-house. It is the property of an old fellow named Harvey, whose house was passed some two miles back, and whose permission is obtained to occupy it for *une piastre* per day.

"Last year Jack and a friend of his both made the trip with me, and they were delighted with the quarters. A good stove and two beds made everything comfortable. The river is just half a mile away, and cannot be seen until the high rocky banks are reached. You suddenly emerge from a little patch of woods, and below you is as grand a scene as can be found in any country. The river flows through an immense cleft in the rocks fully eight hundred to one thousand feet below ; and what a climb it is down the rocks! I won't attempt to describe what it is climbing up again ; I always lose my breath just thinking of it.

"Reaching the river, which seems walled in on all sides by mountains, an old flat-bottomed boat takes you to an island in the centre of the gorge. My companions both forgot that they had come to fish ; they simply stood, looked and wondered "where they were at." The transition from woods and clearing to a wild cañon and rushing river, in the midst of magnificent mountains, was so sudden as to be almost supernatural. One can cast successfully all about the island, with, perhaps, the best success at the head. The fish average large, from three to five pounds, and are very plenty, especially during the last week of the open season.

"Jack claims the ouananiche fight harder here than at any other place, not excepting the Grande Décharge. Be that as it may, one requires much time to rest his wrist after taking two or three fish. At night we made the killing climb up the mountain, and enjoyed a much needed rest at the cabin.

"I neglected to state that all one requires on this trip is the service of one man. He can cook, paddle you to the island, net fish, and especially paddle you about the second pool, that must be fished from a boat. Maurice Boivin, of Metabetchouan Bridge, Mr. Beemer's guardian for the river, I have always taken, and

Third Pool. Metabetchouan River.

found him most excellent. He knows just where the fish lie, and speaks a little English."

"That would please me," Bert again interrupts; "I am disgusted with hearing nothing but French jargon jabbered all the time, that I cannot understand a word of. I can only talk to my men with my hands, and the more I attempt that the less they understand me. All I hear continually repeated is '*Sais pas.*'"

"Jack and his friend went to the second pool the following day, and I went alone to the third again. Jack's description of the day was very good. ' First, the descent to the river is gradual and very easy ; that we appreciated. We found a flat-bottomed scow built of slabs. It was simply nailed together, not caulked at all. With three of us in it, one had to bail every moment. We fished the lower end of the pool, and Boivin would take us close to the big rapid at the foot, as we thought into the danger point, but as we always caught fish just there, we forgot the danger. Anyhow we came out all right. The pool seemed fairly filled with fish ; we counted over fifty jump while taking our lunch at noon. While not quite as wild as the third pool, the scenery is grand. With something better than a clumsy, leaky old scow to fish from, one could be comfortable and save more fish, as you could then easily follow up the long runs that some of them make. We walked about a half mile down the rocks to the first pool. It is a wild, uncanny sort of place, that must be fished from the rocks, which often give a precarious foothold.'

"We remained until the last day of the season, and had splendid success. When we came to leave we had an amusing time settling up with old Harvey. As Jack and his friend did not speak French, the settlement was left to me. The dollar a day for use of the log-cabin was all O. K., but quite a string of extras was added. One for crossing his land, one for a little hay eaten by Gauthier's horses, and one for a few potatoes we had used from a little patch in the clearing. Knowing the old fellow's liking for whiskey, and having had the same trouble in settling before, I tried old methods. As each claim came up, I would take Harvey into the cabin, and fill a glass with a generous portion of whiskey and hand it to him, remarking : '*Pour le chemin*'—'*Pour le foin*' '*Pour les*

palates.'   Between his desire for the drinks and avarice he hesi-
tated but a moment ; the desire was paramount, and in each
instance he replied, '*Oui, M'sieur.*'

"The old man and his wife always come over to the cabin, if
anyone is stopping there, and keep it in perfect condition—make
the beds, wash the dishes, clean out and cut wood.   It is a most
comfortable place to stop, and is well located to reach the three
pools.

"This past year Mr. Beemer closed these pools, allowing no
fishing, as he desired all the ouananiche that could be taken for
the hatchery.   His intentions are hereafter, I believe, to reserve
the third pool only, and leave the others open to guests as
heretofore."

Falls and Ouananiche Pool. Metabetchouan River.

CHAPTER IX.

"What other trips can be made that will afford plenty of fishing and shooting?" Bert asked one evening, after we had had our usual successful day's sport.

"I will have to answer that as your guides do your questions : '*Je ne sais pas.*' Really I do not know. I can tell you of a number, but it would take too much time in which to recount them. Those that you and I have made, and the others I have told you of, have always been so satisfactory to me, that I have often repeated them rather than seek out new ones. In season, which for all birds, moose and caribou opens September 1st, except for ducks on September 15th, almost any trip will afford a possible chance to secure some of them, especially south of Lake St. John, where large game abounds. During the summer one must seek fishing only, unless a bear is expected to be met with, which often occurs. That, of course, can be shot and secured, or shot at and secured—which latter also often occurs. You know, Bert, the old saying, 'What strange things one sees when he does not have a gun.' It is especially true in this country, and a rifle is a good thing to carry along.

"In relating my trips, I have mentioned many additional or side ones that could be taken as well. You will recall, also, when we first reached the lake, that I stated trips could be made from one day to weeks and months in extent. Such, for instance, as a day's trip trout fishing on the Ouiatchouaniche, a day for ouananiche on the Grande Décharge, or two months and a half to Rupert House, James Bay, and return. For trips lasting one, two or three weeks, there are fully fifty that can be easily made within the limit, and all affording grand sport. Three-quarters of them could be well named voyages of discovery, as, aside from the guides, no one has ever made them. It would be very simple to find lakes and rivers new even to the Indians themselves. A trip can be planned in a few moments, almost at random, and always prove satisfactory.

"By ascending either of the three great rivers—the Ashuap-mouchouan, Mistassini or Peribonca—any one of their numerous tributaries can be taken and followed up. As, practically, all of them are of considerable size, each naturally drains a very large area and is the outlet of several lakes. Each lake, in turn, has one or more inlets that come from still other lakes. Practically all of these are virgin, unexplored. Just imagine the magnificent fishing awaiting the seeker! Nor is there any trouble whatever to make any of the trips. One cannot get lost, the Indian guides are too expert and know the general lay of the country too well. You know, Bert, one can always retrace his route if necessary."

"Have none of these tributary rivers been explored by sportsmen?" Bert asks. "It does not seem possible, with the large number who have visited Lake St. John, that these have been overlooked."

"Possibly some that enter the larger rivers near their mouth have been ascended some little distance, but not explored completely. Such rivers as the Little Peribonca, Aleck, Au Foin, or Rat, have probably been ascended in part, but those entering above have not. It would take several ordinary trips to any of these tributary rivers to obtain an understanding regarding them.

"The number of lakes and rivers within the watershed of Lake St. John and emptying into it will never be known; it is very great. An area of one hundred thousand square miles does not encompass them. This, by the way, is about the area controlled by Mr. Beemer in his lease from the Government, and all of which is open to guests of the Hotel Roberval. Don't you think, Bert, that it is ample to accommodate all the sportsmen from the States, and furnish them magnificent sport?"

"There is no question about that, Mac; but many of the trips are too difficult for the average sportsman; there is too much hard work and roughing it about them."

"You are correct, Bert; but to many that adds to sport and makes it more enjoyable. Good fishing, hard to obtain, is always best appreciated. However, I am able to state that Mr. Beemer

A Caribou from Lac de Belle Rivière Country.

intends, in the near future, to remove some of the hardships and difficulties. His idea is to locate two or three comfortable branch hotels, somewhat similar to the Island House, at convenient points on the three large rivers. Access to them will be made as easy as possible. Here, in the midst of the wilderness, with all kinds of fishing about him, the sportsman can locate comfortably and make short or long trips, as he may desire. This will make it possible for many more of the now unknown waters to be found and fished that otherwise could not be, except by the favored few who have unlimited time to devote to sport. Where is there any such preserve in the world, where one can fish without the expense of a special license or paying for the privilege? One who is a guest of the Hotel Roberval finds it all open before him to go where he pleases ; provided, of course, that guides, canoes, camping outfit and provisions are secured from the Roberval Hotel."

" But how about the present law in the Province of Quebec, by which Americans are compelled to pay thirty-five dollars for a first-class license to fish and hunt ? That, I understand, is in full force, and must be taken out yearly. Even in the case of members of any of the fishing clubs, I understand, they must pay half the amount— fifteen dollars."

" That is all true what you state, Bert ; but it does not apply in any way to Lake St. John, or rather Mr. Beemer's preserve surrounding it. Absolutely no license of any kind is needed.

" There is nothing lazy in the make-up of any of the guides in this country. They are always ready and willing to go—no distance seems too far, and no pack too heavy for them to carry. Above all, they are absolutely honest. Even whisky, with their innate love for it, they will never take unless offered to them. They try to anticipate your wants, and are on watch constantly to be of assistance.

" It is a difficult matter, Bert, to do any sort of justice to the subject of what trips one can take in this country. One can treat of it in a general way only. Most of those that I have made myself I have described to you with more or less detail. The others, I have just told you about how much is known concerning them. I can only add—and I think you will agree with me—that this is the

finest country for the sportsman extant. Here fish can always be
caught, and plenty of them. Those who desire to explore entirely
unknown country, and absolutely 'rough it,' can do so to their
heart's content. The only limit is time and endurance."

"How little, comparatively speaking, this country and its
possibilities for sport are known in the States," Bert interposes.
"It does seem to me as though the yearly rush of sportsmen would
be tremendous. Nearly everyone is a sportsman now, you know."

"The inrush of sportsmen now, Bert, is very large, and is
destined to increase many fold. However, there is room for all,
and to spare."

CHAPTER X.

THE HATCHERY.

Bert and I had found such splendid success on our fishing trips that we had taken a longer vacation-time than we had counted on in the beginning. Naturally we were anxious to start for home, but the desire to see Mr. Beemer's latest enterprise—the hatchery—proved too strong, and we decided to remain over a day to visit it. Incidentally, I can say we did not regret our decision. A beautiful drive of five miles through the quaint old village of Roberval, and over a gradually ascending road giving a magnificent view of Lake St. John, brought us to the hatchery. The building is located a short distance back from the road, completely hidden in the hills, that afford it ample protection from the cold lake winds in winter.

We were met by the superintendent, and, thanks to his attention, learned all pertaining to the hatchery and raising of fish. "We have," he advised us, "thousands of trout, salmon and ouananiche in various stages of development, from fry to fingerlings, and we are most successful in raising them. At present we shall not raise many trout, but confine ourselves principally to ouananiche and salmon. We have every facility, and expect to raise immense numbers each year. Our water is the coldest and purest I have ever seen in any hatchery, and the supply more than ample. We have dammed the stream just below, and have a fine pond, in which we are placing the ouananiche as rapidly as we secure them."

Leading the way to the pond, the superintendent took a pole, with a long piece of fine wire attached, to the end of which he fastened a grasshopper, and cast it out on the water. In a moment two or three hungry ouananiche made a dash and jump for the bait, and each cast was a repetition of this. It was a sight that made one's fishing blood tingle, and I did not blame Bert when he said : "Just let me put a fly on the end of that wire. If I could play one of those big fellows, I think I could rest content." It was as tantalizing as anything that ever Tantalus had to undergo. The superintendent stated he expected to have fully two hundred fish in the pond when the spawning time arrived, which was about November 15th.

The hatchery is a two-storey building, about twenty feet by fifty feet, the lower floor being completely filled with hatching and breeding boxes. The water from the brook flows into the upper floor, and, rushing through open troughs, is led by a separate pipe to each box below. A check valve on each pipe controls the force of the water required. The boxes are about four feet long and are arranged in pairs. They are placed end to end, one below the other, the lower receiving the water from the upper. We found all the boxes filled with fish ranging from one inch long to fingerlings of three or four inches. Careful examination failed to discover a single dead fish. The rapid flow of water and the cleanable screens prevent the lodging of any impurities in the boxes. Mashed liver is fed the fish regularly about every two hours, and all particles not taken lodge against the outlet screens, which are quickly removed and cleaned.

Both to Bert and myself it was a surprise to find such a quantity of salmon (*salmo salar*) being raised, and we asked an explanation from the superintendent.

"Mr. Beemer," he replied, "is not only anxious to improve the ouananiche fishing by artificially propagating these fish, but is particularly desirous to afford anglers salmon fishing as well. What few rivers there are in Canada that contain salmon are all under lease, restricting the fishing to a few owners and guests. We believe, and with good reason, that we can place the young salmon in Lake St. John, and in a few years afford fine salmon fishing. By means of the Grande Décharge, whose rapids are not impassable for them, and the Saguenay, they can reach the St. Lawrence and the sea. The greater majority, following their natural instinct, will doubtless do so, but we hope they will return here each year to spawn. It is a peculiarity of the salmon that they always return to the same river where they were hatched and bred. Some of them will remain here permanently, beyond question, not seeking

Portaging the Canoe.

the sea. Thus we will have two chances of having the fish and
fishing. The same experiment has been tried by the Maine fish
commission in that state for several years, and very successfully.
They have many fish that have never gone to the sea, and have
taken some of twelve pounds and over. We shall be equally
successful here."

"From my experience," Bert here remarked, "I consider the
ouananiche a sufficient attraction to draw me to this country. When
that fishing increases from your propagation, I cannot see room for
a desire for anything else."

"Others are not as readily satisfied. With some, trout fishing
is too tame, and, after a day or two, either ouananiche or salmon
fishing palls upon them. But with all kinds of fishing to be had,
satisfaction must ensue. What Mr. Beemer aims to do is to make
the Lake St. John country afford the finest fresh-water fishing in
the world, and I do not question but that he will succeed."

"There can be no question," I replied, "that success will
immediately follow his efforts. Salmon fishing, once established,
will vie with the ouananiche as a drawing attraction. There is one
thing certain, Mr. Beemer can claim that he has the only ouananiche
fishing in the world."

"That is true," the superintendent interrupts, "and he pur-
poses keeping it. He has already been offered large amounts for
fry and spawn, but will never let any go."

"Here the ouananiche is a dweller is rapid waters, rarely
exceeding seven or eight pounds in weight, and then only by a
pound or two ; whereas its cousin of the States, that they are now
beginning to call ouananiche also, is a dead-water fish, grows to
twenty and even twenty-five pounds weight, and lacks much of the
fighting powers of the Lake St. John fish. Environment has had
much to do with it, but the primitive ancestors of both were probably the same. The true ouananiche has become the gamest
fresh-water fish, the other has degenerated to second cousinship.
Do you not agree with me?" I asked, as I concluded.

"I do fully. I have caught both kinds, and there is but little
comparison. I shall take fish only from the very roughest waters
from which to secure spawn, and shall not allow the fish to

deteriorate in any way. We shall raise as many fish as our quarters will allow, so that the fishing, instead of decreasing, will constantly improve."

"Where do you secure your salmon spawn?" Bert asks.

"From the Government salmon-hatchery at Tadousac, at the mouth of the Saguenay. The Government will allow us any quantity we may desire. We shall raise and plant as many as possible of these fish as well. I have had much to contend with in getting the hatchery under successful headway, as we are so far removed from the base of supplies. Everything is running smoothly now, and next year we will run to our fullest capacity. Our facilities for transporting the ouananiche from the pools where they were caught here were very crude, but we lost few fish. My plans are made to perfect this another year.

"From my experience, I believe the establishing of this hatchery was the one thing to be done to make sure the future success of the fishing at Lake St. John. Waters can be overfished, and these would be no exception, with the increasing crowds of visiting fishermen each year. In a short time the fish would become depleted and the attraction would be gone. Now it must increase and afford better sport than ever before. With the added attraction of salmon fishing, I doubt if anyone will ever want to go anywhere else. The hatchery itself will prove a wonderful attraction to visitors. It will be the main point of interest."

I had intended driving to the Ouiatchouan Falls, two miles distant from the hatchery, but the hour was so late it was impossible. "You will have to content yourself, Bert," I remarked, "with the distant view you have had of them from the train and the boat. They are well worthy of a special visit, though. They are between two hundred and fifty and two hundred and seventy feet high, and a large body of water falls in a beautiful sheet, partially broken at two or three points in the descent. Good-sized trout are often taken in the pool below the falls, and when the ice goes out in the spring magnificent ouananiche fishing can be had where the river flows into the lake."

"All one requires in this country is time, nothing but time," Bert wails. "If one had three hundred and sixty-five days to

spend in this wilderness, on the three hundreth and sixty-sixth
day he would find some other place that he wanted to go to badly,
and would know he was just beginning to see a little of this
immense territory. I cannot content myself with the thought of
going home, and seeing those ouananiche in the pond has made
me desire to go back to the Décharge and catch more. But,
seriously, Mac, it is a wise act on Mr. Beemer's part to establish
that hatchery. The expense must have been great, too. His outlay of money in this country must be immense; and when the
country and sport become thoroughly known to American sportsmen, they will seek it in crowds."

"That is certainly true, Bert; I know that his outlay in this
country exceeds three hundred thousand dollars. Everything for
comfort has been done, and now everything to preserve and improve the fishing is being undertaken. Sportsmen will learn of,
seek, and appreciate it. You can see that there is room for all, and
to spare. I am very glad that we remained over to see the hatchery,
as it has not only given us a perfect idea of the hatching and raising
of fish, but shows us that future fine fishing, and the future of the
ouananiche, is assured fully. It was an undertaking requiring
nerve to open this country at such a great expense, and it was
looked upon as a veritable Mulberry Seller's scheme. Its success
is now more than assured; and it is a tenet of my faith that the
last expense—the hatchery—is the greatest improvement of all, and,
beyond question, assures success in return for the great outlay. It
will certainly prove to be a great attraction, also, to sportsmen and
guests of the hotel alike, and forms the greatest addition to the
large list of attractions here."

CHAPTER XI.

THE SAGUENAY.

No matter how many times it may be made, one can never tire of the Saguenay river route from Chicoutimi to Tadousac, and thence up the broad St. Lawrence to Quebec. While the entire trip from Roberval, including the initial rail journey, the uncertain delay at Chicoutimi, and the boat trip from there, occupies two nights and a day; no matter how much one may be pressed for time, it is the mistake of a lifetime not to make it. There is absolutely no exaggeration contained in the statement that there is not a steamboat trip to be found elsewhere that can, in full measure, favorably compare with the seventy miles of indescribable grandeur of scenery bordering the mysterious Saguenay. Bert accepted my advice to return that way, especially from having a desire to see the Government salmon-hatchery at Tadousac. At 7.30 P. M. we bade good-bye to Roberval, and were *en route* for Chicoutimi. The journey occupied something over two hours, our destination being reached before 10 P. M.

Chicoutimi is well worthy of a stop-over for a day or more, offering much of interest to the visitor. Formerly the hotel accommodations were very poor, but, fortunately, a new modern hotel—the Château Saguenay—has recently been built, that is a model hostelry in every way. It is reached by a flight of steps from the train. Here we are to remain for the night, or for such portion of it as the fates, or rather the tide, decrees.

The tide at Chicoutimi, the head of navigation on the Saguenay, has very irregular hours for making its rise of nine feet. The steamers must come and go with its flood, which may occur at any hour from 3 A. M. until noon the next day. One will do well to engage the hotel porter to secure staterooms on the boat, at once upon its arrival, as reservations cannot be made in advance.

Bert and I left at 6 A. M., a fairly respectable hour. We were fortunate in that it was the "Carolina's" trip, she being the best of the fleet, although the others, even the old "Saguenay," are very comfortable.

Island House, Grande Décharge.

A few miles below Chicoutimi the wonderful scenery of the river first comes into view; therefore, breakfast should be gotten early, in order that none of it may be unseen. Within half an hour after starting, two immense mountains, located on either side of the river, dimly appear in the distance. In answer to Bert's inquiry, I informed him that they were, respectively, Capes East and West; the latter guarding the entrance to Ha! Ha! Bay, which opens out from the river twelve miles below Chicoutimi. If the tide is late, the trip up this bay is made coming up; if early, on the return. Nine miles up, the little town of St. Alphonse is at the head of the bay, where enter two little salmon rivers—the Ha! Ha! and Mars. Both are under lease to the Messrs. Price, the lumber kings of this region.

After our picturesque trip up the bay, we are again in the river, and the number of high, rugged and grand masses of mountains, on either side, increases rapidly. Some six or eight miles below, a notable piece of Nature's handiwork is seen. Located on the south shore is a sheer precipice of rock ascending directly from the water to a height of, apparently, six or seven hundred feet. Viewed from a distance, it seems absolutely vertical and smooth. Appropriately, it is named " Le Tableau " (the picture).

Fortune had favored us with a beautiful day and clear atmosphere, enabling us to see everything distinctly. Bert kept his eyes roving constantly, missing nothing. Every rock a trifle higher than its neighbor, he claimed, must, properly, have a name, and plied me with incessant questions as to what the names were. Desiring to satisfy his curiosity in some way, I applied any peculiar French name that came to mind, followed by some odd translation that I could conjure up on the moment. I can still recall his remark, "The French people can dig up the most peculiar and unsuitable names imaginable."

Now, in the distance, can be seen two immense mountains rearing themselves high above all others. So magnificent is the sight that with our gradual approach, which brings each new detail into view, one wishes the boat would stop and permit the eye to feast upon it from that one spot. These are the wonderful Capes Trinity and Eternity. How fittingly both are named the former, three immense rounded peaks, apparently separated, yet all one. Nothing that Nature has made, that eye can see, could more appropriately be named in commemoration of the Divine Trinity. Nearly two thousand feet this great mountain rises, with fully one thousand feet absolutely sheer from the water—grand in its superb mightiness, grand in its solitude, awe-inspiring that its foot is washed by the waters in the mysterious depths two thousand feet below. High upon the terraced summit has been placed, emblematically and appropriately, a cross, fifty feet high, yet so far above is it that it does not appear more than a fraction of that height. Closely the steamer approaches the wall of rock, and, as compared with it, we are but a speck upon the waters. With such awe-inspiring surroundings, one cannot but contrast and think that the greatest monuments of man's handiwork and the monuments erected by Nature would not compare even as favorably as did our steamer with magnificent Trinity.

As we approach the precipitous sides and parallel them closely, a large bucket of stones is placed on the deck for the passengers to test their ability to hit a large mark. It seems so easy, you naturally try, and you fall far short. The immense height of the rock so near makes the distance deceptive. Apparently you are not over one hundred feet distant, in reality you are several times that.

Rounding Cape Trinity, the steamer enters Eternity Bay, and beside us stands Cape Eternity, grand yet sombre in its immensity. One large mass of rock, with but little irregularity, it also rises sheer from the immense depths. How far back into the past and with what terrific convulsion of nature were these magnificent mountains erected? Man cannot tell, nor can he know through how many ages to come they will stand sentinel over the mysterious river at their feet.

The steamer makes the circuit of the bay, and at frequent intervals the whistle is blown to show the numerous echoes as the sound reverberates from mountain to mountain until lost. Fully six or seven distinct repetitions of the sound are heard. We are now about forty miles from the St. Lawrence, and, while the highest mountains have been passed, the scenery of the balance of the trip is grand in the extreme. It is one continuous succession of rocky points and mountain-surrounded bays about and through which the river winds.

One naturally asks : is the Saguenay a river? Unfathomable are its depths in many places, and but a few feet distant from the base of Capes Trinity and Eternity a depth of over two thousand feet has been found. So much deeper is it than the St. Lawrence, that, it is stated, were that river to become dry the Saguenay would still have two-thirds or more of its depth remaining. Some great convulsion of Nature, that must have shaken the world, cleft the Laurentian mountains, hurling them apart, into which the waters rushed. True, it has a current, and is the outlet of Lake St. John ; but could it not be as properly termed a lake or bay?

Ten miles below Eternity Bay, the Little Saguenay enters from the south, a river almost the counterpart of the larger in point of magnificent scenery, and especially noted for its splendid trout fishing. Two large islands are next passed, each ranging from one and a half to two miles long. Then, twelve miles from Tadousac, the noted salmon river, the Marguerite, enters from the north. More towering mountains of rugged formation are passed ; La Boule Point, that seems for a time to bar our further progress, is left behind. Now can be seen the immense promontories, Pointe-aux-Vaches and Pointe-aux-Bouleaux, that so fittingly stand sentinel over the Saguenay waters as they mingle with the St. Lawrence.

The steamer ties up at the wharf at Tadousac, which is located on the north shore just at the point where the rivers join, and a stop of two hours is usually made. But a few steps distant, in a large natural basin in the rock connected with the river, is the salmon-pool connected with the Government hatchery, and in which the fish are kept until ripe for spawning. The tide is out, leaving but four or five feet of clear water in the pool, permitting the salmon to be distinctly seen. A large number of fish can always be found swimming around and occasionally leaping from the water. These have been secured by netting at various points on the lower St. Lawrence. Magnificent great fellows they are, ranging from fifteen to twenty pounds to certainly fifty or sixty. Bert finally said : " I would not hesitate to trangress every law and stand any punishment to be able to catch one of these big ones. If I had a rod and cast, I think I would try at that." I could only reply : " There are others, too, that feel as you do, Bert?"

I believe he would have stood there for hours had I not gotten him away to see the hatchery. This is located but a short distance up the road, but, unfortunately for us, was not in operation, as the fish were not ripe for spawning. We went through the buildings, however, and found them very completely fitted for the purpose ; similar in many respects to the hatchery at Roberval, only on a much larger scale.

From the hatchery we walked about half a mile to the village, where I wanted to show Bert the site of the first church built in Canada. The original Jesuit mission was built here in 1648, and the small building now standing in 1750. Visitors are shown parts of the skull and coffin of the first missionary, which, it is claimed, were found in taking down the original building. Tadousac was first visited by Jacques Cartier as early as 1535.

I can only repeat, that no one who visits Lake St. John can afford to miss the Saguenay route on the return to Quebec. Aside from the unsurpassed scenery, the historical interest is engrossing, since about here it was that the very earliest history of Quebec was made. No one with sporting blood in his veins should miss seeing the magnificent salmon—the king of all fish ; neither will one have any regret travelling hundreds of miles to see this spot, except that he cannot try his flies if only on one fish.

Leaving Tadousac, the steamer crosses the St. Lawrence—which at this point is twenty-two miles wide—diagonally, a distance of twenty-eight miles to Rivière-du-Loup wharf, the landing-place for the town of the same name as well as Cacouna, the great Canadian watering-place, situated four miles below.

The steamer had proceeded some distance when Bert asked : "What are those round sand-hills we see so numerous about Tadousac? They are very peculiar."

"An interesting answer can be given to your question, Bert. They are called Mamelons, and the Montagnais Indian name for them is Tadousac. Geologists claim that at one time they formed the shore of the ocean, and were worn into their present shape as

Indian Guides preparing Dinner.

the waters gradually receded. Nothing else could have made them
as they are, or could account for the sea-sand being there. About
them is woven the history of the Montagnais Indians, once the most
powerful tribe on the continent, now reduced in numbers to a few
hundred. They did much towards making Canadian history, and
wonderful and beautiful are their traditions. Their history is the
history of the Mamelons from time immemorial. Here hundreds
of generations of the tribe came and have passed away ; and when
final extinction comes, as it is fated it must, the history of the
Montagnais will not fade from memory while the countless sands
of the Mamelons remain one upon the other—their monument.''

As is usual here in crossing the St. Lawrence, we saw a number of grampus, seals and white porpoises. Some of them we
could easily have shot from the steamer. After a short stop at
Rivière-du-Loup, a two-hours' sail brought us to Murray Bay,
another well-known summer resort. A stay of two hours enabled
us to view the magnificent new hotel and the large number of
beautiful cottages that make up the summer town. At 10 o'clock
the boat started for its all-night trip to Quebec. Thoroughly tired
after our long day of sight-seeing, we gladly sought our berths for
needed rest. Arising early, we find we are just approaching grand,
old, historic Quebec—the Gibraltar of Canada. Quaint and old,
the city takes pride in its great antiquity. Modern only in her
public buildings, in the new residences in the outskirts, new city
gates, and the magnificent hotel, the Château Frontenac; ancient in
the same narrow streets, the same little houses, the same ramparts,
walls and citadel, still remaining, that witnessed the defeats and
victories of Wolfe, Montcalm and Montgomery. Easily can the
visitor find much that will recall the earlier noted men in Canada's
infancy—Frontenac and Champlain.

The eager sportsman, *en route* to Lake St. John, is always in
too great a hurry to engage in his favorite sport to stop in Quebec
going ; but he makes a great mistake if he does not remain over a
day at least, returning. There is so much to see in and about the
city of more than passing interest, the day passes leaving much
unseen, and one departs with deep regret that more time was not
given to the stay in Quebec.

CHAPTER XII.

"There is so much diversity of opinion now-a-days, Bert, in reference to tackle, rods, guns, etc., that it is not well to undertake advising a sportsman what to take for use in the Lake St. John country. Such advice provokes a discussion at once, ending in both retaining their individual opinions, as is the result in talking politics. When approached on the subject, I invariably reply that I do not know, that I can only state what I prefer to use."

"You are entirely correct in that statement," Bert replied, "and I agree with you in your ideas. I have never, in my experience, seen so many fishermen as I have met with on this trip who should have had some advice in advance in regard to what tackle to use. A man can strike and land a half-pound trout or a three-pound ouananiche with an eighteen-foot, two-handed, heavy salmon rod, and be content, from the fact that he has the fish; but the sport is lacking."

"Yes; and he can hook and play a heavy ouananiche or salmon—possibly—with a four-ounce rod," I reply. "He has sport, so much that it grows monotonous as he becomes exhausted. He has the fish as a result—perhaps."

Bert and I talked over this subject thoroughly during our trip down the Saguenay, and I can say that we agreed perfectly.

The question of rods is of paramount importance; therefore, it is best to state what the concensus of opinion of the majority of ouananiche fishermen is, rather than to exploit individual ideas and preferences. A split bamboo rod of fine—not cheap—make is the favorite at long odds. Lancewood, greenheart or bethabara have a very few advocates. Lightness compatible with strength is first considered, while a suitable length for something over medium distance casting—say nine and one-half or ten feet—is correct. Individual preference properly governs the weight, but it should not be below five and one-half nor exceed eight ounces.

I have known two or three extremists who always use rods from three and a half to four and a half ounces for ouananiche. It was a constant struggle to save the rod, to save the fish, and to try and save the wrist; but, after playing a single one, the member in question had to be laid up for repairs. The other extreme—too heavy a rod—prohibits proper playing, and many fish are naturally lost

To properly play such a hard-fighting fish as is the ouananiche a light, springy rod is absolutely necessary. These fish are most frequently hooked lightly, rarely gorging the hook, as does the trout or bass. In this respect they are much like their ancestor, the salmon. As they usually take the fly in rough or foamy water—their natural abiding place—the strike is not always seen, and a good strike in return, to set the hook, cannot be made with safety. The better chance for success lies in always considering the fish to be lightly hooked. A light, springy rod aids much in keeping the line taut, preventing slack, while the spring tires the fish much more quickly. From five and a half to seven ounces are considered to be the best weights. The ouananiche is a tackle-smashing fish, no matter how carefully handled; therefore, two or three rods, at least, should be included in one's equipment. A modern way of carrying two rods in a small compass is to have two second joints and four tips fitted to one butt; breakage is therefore provided for.

Bert says, "By all means recommend the automatic reel," and I do. When the fish makes its furious run, every effort must be made to avoid a slack line. One hand should be free to manipulate it and ease it when the fish jumps. This cannot be done when one is engaged in turning a crank in a fruitless endeavor to reel in the slack as fast as the fish gives it. The little finger of the rod-hand releases the spring of the automatic reel, allowing it to take slack as fast as given. The other hand is free to draw out a yard or more of line when the fish is not running, and given and taken in when it jumps, to keep the strain equal. Good, heavy, six-foot loop trout-leaders are the best, but one must be sure that they are good. An "E" enamelled silk line I believe to be absolutely the best kind and size to use. Another special advantage of

this tackle I have described, and the flies I will mention, is that
all are equally adapted for trout fishing.

Just here I will quote a parody on some well-known lines that
I sprung upon Bert one evening, when we had seen some fishermen casting small spoons and phantom minnows for ouananiche in
the Grande Décharge. It will illustrate what I wish to say.

> " What bait do you use?" I ask of another
>   Who has a large catch, and my sport is slow.
> " Flies only," he answers, "my angling brother;
>   There's no better bait, I'll swear, that I know."
> " Best for sportsmanlike use," I say; "but, ah ! when
>   You cast hours, no luck, what then?"
>   'Tis a thing I hate,
>   His lying about bait,
> When his flies were some cute little spoons.

There is nothing in the law to prohibit the use of spinners,
spoons, phantom minnows or lake bait in fishing for ouananiche ;
but there is an unwritten sportsman's law which would read :
" Use flies, nothing else." One should by all means be supplied
with some large spoons and a trolling-line for pike-perch and
pike—but leave them behind when out for ouananiche. Give the
fish an equal chance—match skill and light tackle against game,
hard-fighting instinct. Supposing that four pounds of fish outwits
two hundred or more pounds of man, one feels much better than
to haul in a fish with both jaws locked together with a gang of
hooks that calls for an expenditure of time and cuss words to
unhook. One is sport—the other lacks even the first element of it.
Why not have a bell ring when the fish bites, then touch a button
and have an electric winch wind it in ; in the meantime read a
book—there will be no interruption in an exciting passage. True,
when fish have an off day and won't take the fly, one is sorely
tempted to try a spoon. Resist the temptation, you will feel better
for it ; to-morrow they will take the fly.

In the matter of flies there is much diversity of opinion, not so
much, perhaps, as to kind, but more particularly as to the size best
adapted for ouananiche. Many will claim that large sizes, such as
Nos. 1, 2 and 3, are the best ; still others advocate sizes all along

from No. 5 to No. 8; the great majority, however, claiming—and properly, too—that Nos. 4, 5 and 6 are the most successful. After twelve years' experience, I agree with the majority, and confine myself to Nos. 4 and 5. I have met one or two extremists, no more, that make great claims for Nos. 10 and 12. They belong to the same class that prefer a three and a half ounce rod. I will guarantee that any experienced ouananiche fisher will not only attract more fish with a No. 5 fly, but that he will bring safely to net three or more fish to the extremist's one. So much for size— now for kind.

The "Jock Scott" and "Silver Doctor" are undoubtedly the leaders. The "McCarthy Ouananiche," something of a cross between the two, is usually successful. The "B. A. Scott," "General Hooker," "Hare's Ear," "Professor," "Queen of the Water," "Brown Hackle" and "Coachman" are all very good. With plenty of these in one's fly-book, all vagaries of the ouananiche appetite is provided for. I have taken these fish on all manner of flies, in all kinds of weather. I have had at times a "White Miller," a "Parmacheene Belle," a "Yellow Sally," and even a "Scarlet Ibis" taken as freely as any other, but they cannot be recommended. For trout, the same size and kinds of flies are proper. In the virgin trout waters they seem to take almost anything that looks like a fly, but the very best of all for *fontinalis* is the "Parmacheene Belle" and "Scarlet Ibis."

Especial care should be taken in selecting a landing-net. One with a five or six-foot handle and with the net proper fully thirty inches deep is required. Either from the canoe or from the rocks, long reaches must be often made to net a fish. Then, too, if not of sufficient depth, an ouananiche, in its jumps, twists and turns, is more than liable to leap out. Another important point is to have the net with an opening diameter of at least eighteen or twenty inches.

Unless one specially desires to hunt small game, a shotgun should not be taken, only a rifle. Large game is to be had, and it is necessary to be prepared for it. I do not desire to start a controversy on the subject, so will not recommend any special kind I will only state that, with many years' experience, I prefer, individually, the 44.40 Winchester, since I have never had it fail me on any game.

Another adjunct to a sportsman's kit, and a very necessary one, is a repellant for flies and mosquitoes—the *bête noire* of the sportsman. The moment one enters the woods, a swarm surrounds and welcomes, and their attacks make life unendurable. Pennyroyal and citronella are especially good, but, being very volatile, must be constantly applied. In an extremity, fat pork rubbed on face and hands is excellent. The very best repellant is pure tar and vaseline—two-thirds of the former and one-third of the latter, well mixed. But one or two applications a day are necessary to give perfect immunity, unless one perspires freely. It becomes hard in a few moments, will not rub off as does tar-oil, scarcely discolors the skin, and washes off easily with cold water. Not only is it a repellant of flies and mosquitoes—the only perfect one I have ever found—but another point in its favor is, that it does not melt and cannot spill out. On this account, a wide-mouth bottle should be used, otherwise it cannot be readily removed.

Of the greatest value in the woods is a rubber poncho or blanket. I do not refer to the small ones ordinarily on sale, but a simple and cheap one, easily obtained. Purchase three yards of light weight imitation rubber carriage-cloth, fifty inches wide, and cut a slit in the centre just sufficiently large to allow the head to pass through. In travelling through the woods or in a canoe, one can put this on and spend hours in the heaviest rain without getting wet. As the sides are open, the wearer does not get heated as with a rubber coat, and, being larger, it gives more protection to the feet and legs. At night it is used as a blanket, placed rubber side down over the bough-bed, to prevent the dampness coming through. It can also be used to make a temporary tent or shelter, if necessary. The total expense of this should not exceed one dollar and a half.

Especially, do not overlook a No. 2 square rubber air-cushion. Sitting all day in a canoe demands this for comfort, as one's seat is the hard bottom of the craft. It can be used as a life-preserver in an emergency, and is especially convenient as a pillow in camp at night.

A tackle-box—leather-covered is preferred—should be carried to contain, in a compact form, all small articles of tackle. Nothing can then be lost, and ready at hand when wanted are reels, fly-hook, leaders, lines, swivels, spoons, trolling-lines, sinkers, hooks of all kinds, net, leader-box, fish-scale, rule for measuring fish, memorandum-book and pencil, and bottle of tar and vaseline. Also, for repairs, it should contain : tool-handle and tools, a strong pocket-knife, oil-can and small bottle of oil, plyers, winding-silk, varnish and brush, needles and thread, and, finally, some court-plaster, quinine, and a bottle of diarrhœa medicine. With this, one is prepared for almost any emergency that may arise.

A hint in regard to necessary clothing and foot covering cannot be amiss. Although two hundred miles north of Quebec, the temperature during the fishing season will be found to vary but little from that of New York State. The days are warm, but the nights are usually cold. Heavy undergarments, with the same outer clothing that one is accustomed to wear in the Adirondacks, will be found thoroughly suitable. Shoes are useless, boots are absolutely necessary, as one must be in the water very frequently. Rubber boots would scarcely last during one day's tramp through the woods or over the rocks. Any good sportsman's high boots—eighteen inches—are suitable, but I can especially recommend either the *bottes sauvages* or *bottes françaises*, that are worn exclusively by the Indians, natives and guides. The former are made comfortable by inserting a heavy birch-bark insole, they being simply a leather moccasin with a high leather top. The latter are made in the same manner, with the addition of a sole and heel to protect the foot from injury. Properly oiled, both are absolutely waterproof. They can be obtained at Quebec or Roberval at an expense of from three to five dollars.

The foregoing describes in a general way what one should carry to be thoroughly prepared for both hunting and fishing in the Lake St. John region. Individual ideas and requirements can supply any further additions that may seem necessary. Avoid useless impedimenta, go into the woods as lightly equipped as possible.

CHAPTER XIII.

My friend Bert has since made a number of trips to Lake St. John, for the reason, as he states, that his first visit, which I have described, afforded him only a morsel to satiate a large appetite for sport. Now that he knows the country, he is able to appease his hunger, at least until the next season rolls around. We often meet and devote the time to recounting our experiences and comparing notes. He has frequently made a remark that I recall, since it contained a suggestion which I have endeavoured to carry out.

"You have doubtless noticed many times, Mac, as have I, how important it is that sportsmen should know just what to take with them to Lake St. John, just what necessary things will be furnished them there, and just where to go when the country is reached. When you write another book, embody all this information in it."

"To my mind, Bert," I have answered, "the 'where to go' subject would offer a difficult, or rather impossible, task to carry out. The total number of trips that we have made together, added to those which each has taken alone, as compared with the number that can be made, is infinitesimal. I could not do that particular subject justice. As to giving general information and describing what tackle to take, that would be comparatively easy."

The trips that have been described, in both a particular and general way, are equally as satisfactory to take now, and afford fully as good sport as they have done in the past. The best suggestion that can be made to the sportsman intending to visit this region is to advise that he write in advance to the Hotel Roberval and engage a good guide. Upon arrival there, he could suggest the kind of trip he desires and the length of time at his command to devote to it. Based upon this, his guide would readily be able to plan one or a series that should afford absolutely satisfying sport. Owing to the large number of sportsmen at Lake St. John during the season, it is much the better and safer plan to engage a good guide in advance, as stated. Do not attempt to select a trip until it can be done in person. This does not entail any delay, since all arrangements can be completed in a few hours after arrival. The adoption of this plan will prevent disappointment, and often vexatious delays as well.

In passing from the States over the border into Canada, one must avoid any trouble with His Majesty's Customs. This can be provided for by taking nothing but actual necessities, such as I have noted. Upon these duties are not exacted, unless possibly when guns are in question, on which a deposit is often required. This is returned when the weapon is taken out of the country. The average Customs officer is a good fellow. He appreciates the fact that sportsmen visit Canada for sport, not to smuggle, and he knows, too, that American dollars are very welcome to his countrymen. This prevents his being over-particular or exacting. In returning to the States, another Customs gauntlet, that of Uncle Sam, is run, and a very particular one it is. One is entitled to take in one hundred dollars value in new clothing and furs (except sealskin). Any other purchases should be declared, and, unless of specific value, no duty will be exacted.

The Hotel Roberval furnishes everything necessary for a camping trip. For this reason, absolutely no attention need be paid to this part of one's outfit, until arrival there and a trip has been planned. Included are tents, blankets, pillows, towels, together with cooking and eating implements contained in a large kettle, and a full complement of provisions, both staple and fancy. A long list of eatables is presented, from which an as elaborate a choice may be made as fancy might dictate.

Each member of a party is furnished with a canoe and two guides. Three-fathom (eighteen feet) canoes are used, which permit a goodly amount of the baggage to be taken in each. Two guides are required, in order to not only expedite and lighten the trip, but especially are they needed in ascending the strong current of the rivers, and to handle the craft safely in running the many rapids.

The Hotel Roberval makes a fixed charge per diem, which covers every expense, including board, use of camp outfit, pay of guides, etc. This charge is quite a little less than the expense for like services would be, with only one guide, in the Adirondacks. Especially reasonable are the rates for board for those who prefer to make only occasional day trips. Prices range from $3.00 to $5.00 per day, or $17.50 to $28.00 per week. Charges at the Island House, in the Grande Décharge, are uniformly $3 00 per day or $17.50 per week. A canoe, with two guides, for fishing, at this point, costs $4.00, including their board.

The question is often asked as to whether the Indian, half-breed and *habitant* guides are wholly reliable and honest. It is a great pleasure to state that they are absolutely so, without a single exception that I now recall. I can quote from my own experience, and add it to that of a large number of others to whom I have put the question, being anxious to learn thoroughly regarding the fact. As is well known, all of these people are especially fond of the whiteman's "firewater." Yet they may be trusted with all that a party may carry, not only with the unopened bottles, but those partially empty as well. Rest assured, however, that a second invitation to indulge is never necessary. Those who are familiar with the Lake St. John guides, and who have employed as well those found in Maine, the Adirondacks and other kindred places, all, without exception, unite in declaring that the former are by far the most willing, and the greatest workers as well, that they have ever found. All of these men speak French—their natural tongue—and many have picked up a few words of English, seeming to understand what is said to them. Usually one guide at least can generally be found in each party who can speak and understand English very well. Some knowledge of French, however, is of great value to the sportsman. It is well to know at once what is meant when the guide hurriedly whispers " L'orignal ici ! " (a moose here). Otherwise the animal might disappear and leave several miles behind him, before the remark was finally interpreted and understood.

To others than those resident in the Province of Quebec, the fish and game laws of that section of Canada are almost unknown,

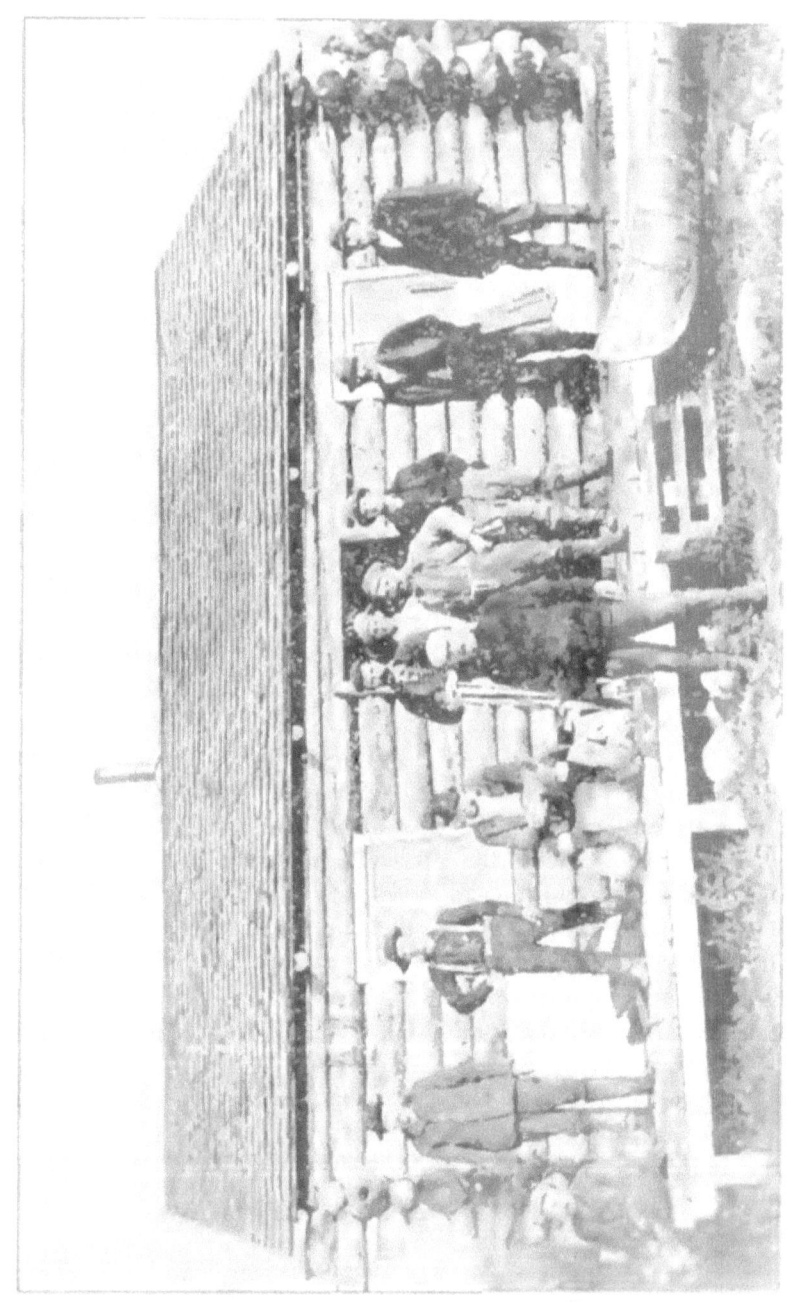

Group of Sportsmen and Guides.

although a knowledge of them is most important. The laws in force in the Province of Ontario, as well as those in Nova Scotia, New Brunswick and Newfoundland, all vary in many material points from those of Quebec. As it is not necessary, however, to write in regard to any except the latter mentioned, the former may be omitted.

Quebec is divided into two sections or zones, designated as Zones Nos. 1 and 2; the former comprising all of the Province located west and south of the Saguenay River; the other, that part lying north and east. There is some variance in the laws of these two sections, but an understanding of the former only is necessary.

The open seasons in Quebec are much more liberal in respect to length than are those of other portions of Canada, and especially of the States. However, the close seasons are of sufficient duration to amply protect both fish and game during their times of reproduction. A determined effort is being made on the part of the Government to enforce these laws strictly, but it is impossible to guard or protect the immense tracts of wilderness far remote from civilization. It devolves, therefore, upon every sportsman to be his own individual warden, and if he be a true knight of the gun and rod, he will prove to be a very strict one. One must respect the rights of others, as well as one's own, by providing for future sport through present protection.

The full list of close seasons for fish and game, including all changes made in 1902, are now as follows:

FISHING.

Salmon—From August 15th to February 1st.

Ouananiche—From September 15th to December 1st.

Speckled trout (*Salmo fontinalis*)—From October 1st to May 1st.

Large grey trout, lake trout, touladi—From October 15th to December 1st.

Pickerel—From April 15th to May 15th.

Bass—From April 15th to June 15th.

Maskinongé—From May 25th to July 1st.

HUNTING.

Caribou—From February 1st to September 1st.

Deer and moose—From January 1st to September 1st.

(During one season, but one moose, two caribou or two deer can be taken.   Fawns and cow moose cannot be killed.)

Beaver—Close season to November 1st, 1905.

Mink, otter, martin—April 1st to November 1st.

Hare—From February 1st to November 1st.

Bear—From July 1st to August 20th.

Muskrat—From May 1st to April 1st.

Woodcock, snipe, plover—From February 1st to September 1st.

Birch or spruce partridge—From December 15th to September 1st.

White partridge or ptarmigan—From February 1st to November 1st.

Wild duck—March 1st to September 15th.

All non-residents of the Province of Quebec are compelled by law to secure fishing and hunting licenses in advance.   This applies to all except a member of any game club, individual lessee, or a guest of either.   As previously stated, Mr. Beemer leases or controls much of the country about Lake St. John and its tributary rivers ; consequently, guests of the Hotel Roberval are his guests, and therefore do not require a license.

To the thorough, all-around sportsman who desires to seek hunting and fishing combined, no time in the year will appeal to him more strongly than will the month of September, for his outing trip about Lake St. John.   The shooting season opens on the first of this month, while that for trout extends to the first of October, and for ouananiche to the fifteenth of September. With the advent of September, winged pests have gone, therefore, immunity from their stings can be had.

While the open time for fishing is on, satisfying sport can be had by seeking the fish where changes in temperature and other conditions force them to go.   In their natural waters, trout are always plentiful in the many rivers and lakes.   They are found running wild and in moderate depths, from the time the ice goes out during May until, with the warming of the water as the season advances to summer and autumn, they seek the coolness of the depths and *l'eau froide* or spring holes. With a slight knowledge of the varying homes of the trout, which as stated constantly change with the seasonable variations of temperature of air and water, one should never be disappointed in the catches that can be made. In fact, in a great majority of cases, many more trout can be taken in a short space of time, than a party with their guides can possibly dispose of. It scarcely seems necessary to advise sportsmen to kill no greater number of fish than can be legitimately used; yet often, too often indeed, large strings are taken simply that they may be photographed to prove one's fish stories and prowess with the rod. If only such fish are kept as may be badly injured with the hook, one can fish until satisfied or exhausted, provided the others are carefully returned to the water. This does not cause the slightest injury, provided the hook is removed with care, and the hand kept wet when handling the fish.

While the ouananiche may be taken at almost all its usual haunts about Lake St. John, and at all times during the season, each locality, naturally, has a specified period when it offers especially good fishing. For a space of two or three weeks immediately following the going out of the ice, magnificent sport can be had in the mouths of the various rivers flowing into the lake. This is especially true of the Ouiatchouan and Metabetchouan. From the middle of June until early in August, the sport at the Grande Décharge is at its best. During August, better catches are made and larger fish taken at the pools adjacent to the many falls and rapids of the Peribonca, Mistassini and Ashuapmouchouan rivers. The ouananiche are then ascending to the spawning beds far above. Many of these fish constantly inhabit the Décharge and make it their spawning bed as well, for which reason more or less satisfying sport is always to be found there.

It is to be understood that very high or very low conditions of the water may add to or detract from one's success. Then, of necessity dependence must be placed in the guides, and if time permits they can seek other places more remote where unfavorable conditions do not exist. All throughout the season of 1901, the water in Lake St. John and its tributaries was at an unprecedently low stage, making the fishing at nearly all points extremely poor. During other seasons or parts of them, high water has materially interfered with success. That vast numbers of ouananiche inhabit the waters of the Lake St. John country no one will deny, but that weather and water conditions will always be just right, or that the element of good luck will attend, cannot be promised.

CHAPTER XIV.

THE PRO AND CON. OF SUCCESS AND SATISFACTION TO BE FOUND.

Since ouananiche fishing has become generally and popularly known, there have been occasional fishermen who were unfortunate in meeting with more or less disappointment in making their initial trip to Lake St. John. That such ill-fortune has befallen them is true, and being made known has unquestionably deterred others from making the trip. These disappointments have arisen from a variety of causes, almost exclusively amongst which is the main one—the fault of the sportsman himself. This, naturally, he cannot and will not see, and therefore does not admit. It is well, for this reason, to analyze the causes carefully.

Primarily, the almost universal idea prevalent with those about to make their first visit, seems to be that one may secure ouananiche and trout fishing, and in fact all manner of sport, with wonderful results, almost at the threshold of the Hotel. It follows, unfortunately that, basing upon this belief, a flying trip is usually planned and made. This may chance to be just at a time when the fish do not happen to take hold freely.

It might be well to state here, that Lake St. John fish are in this respect exactly similar to those of all other localities. All fish have their off day or days, owing either to water or weather changes, a sudden over-supply of food, or from some strange vagary of their nature — inexplicable. Being pressed for time, unable to await the pleasure of the fish or to seek them at more remote points in the surrounding wilderness, the hurried, would-be angler proclaims the possibilities of sport to be exaggerated, unreliable, in fact very poor.

Again, if a trip is planned back into the wilds, and reliance placed upon personal knowledge of journeys supposedly similar, previously taken in the semi-settled wooded portions of Pennsylvania, New York, or Maine, for suitable advance preparations, they will not be suitable for this region. Often indeed, no inquiry whatever is made beforehand as to what is to be expected, and the seeker for sport is totally unprepared to meet or undergo the natural difficulties and hardships. This brings about not only a hurried ending of the jaunt, but also renders it unpleasant to such a degree that the lack of sport is magnified, and an amount satisfying under other conditions, is unsatisfactory.

One may have a too highly colored or exaggerated idea of the fighting powers of the ouananiche, of the vast numbers of these fish and trout to be taken, and quantities of game to be found in this country. Naturally, therefore, he will be greatly disappointed when his high ideals fall down to a point within the range of reason. The ouananiche, while being a prodigy as a fighter, cannot perform all of the wonderful leaping and fighting acts often accredited to it; feats that would require a high-geared engine to furnish the power for.

Other reasons for non-success, such as the use of unsuitable tackle, or lack of knowledge of how to fish, might be added. To know the habits of the fish to be angled for, and something as well of the methods and tackle to be used, is especially necessary for success. If one goes fishing as a novice, he must expect to find satisfying sport only after study and practice, unless he expects to meet with the wonderful luck that sometimes attends the first efforts of a tyro.

It is better to mention these usual causes of disappointments, in order that one may know that such things do occur under certain conditions. It is well also to state that there are always possibilities of many kinds which may arise to cause realization to fall far below one's expectation. Discouragement should not follow — anticipate better success next time. From a number of letters received bearing upon this particular subject, I have selected one which I reproduce in full below. It aptly illustrates the amount of ill-fortune that is sometimes apportioned out to mortals in search of pleasure and sport.

"Should these lines reach you, I feel sure you will pardon my presumption in addressing a stranger, for the sake of a common bond of angling experience, which 'makes us wondrous kind.'

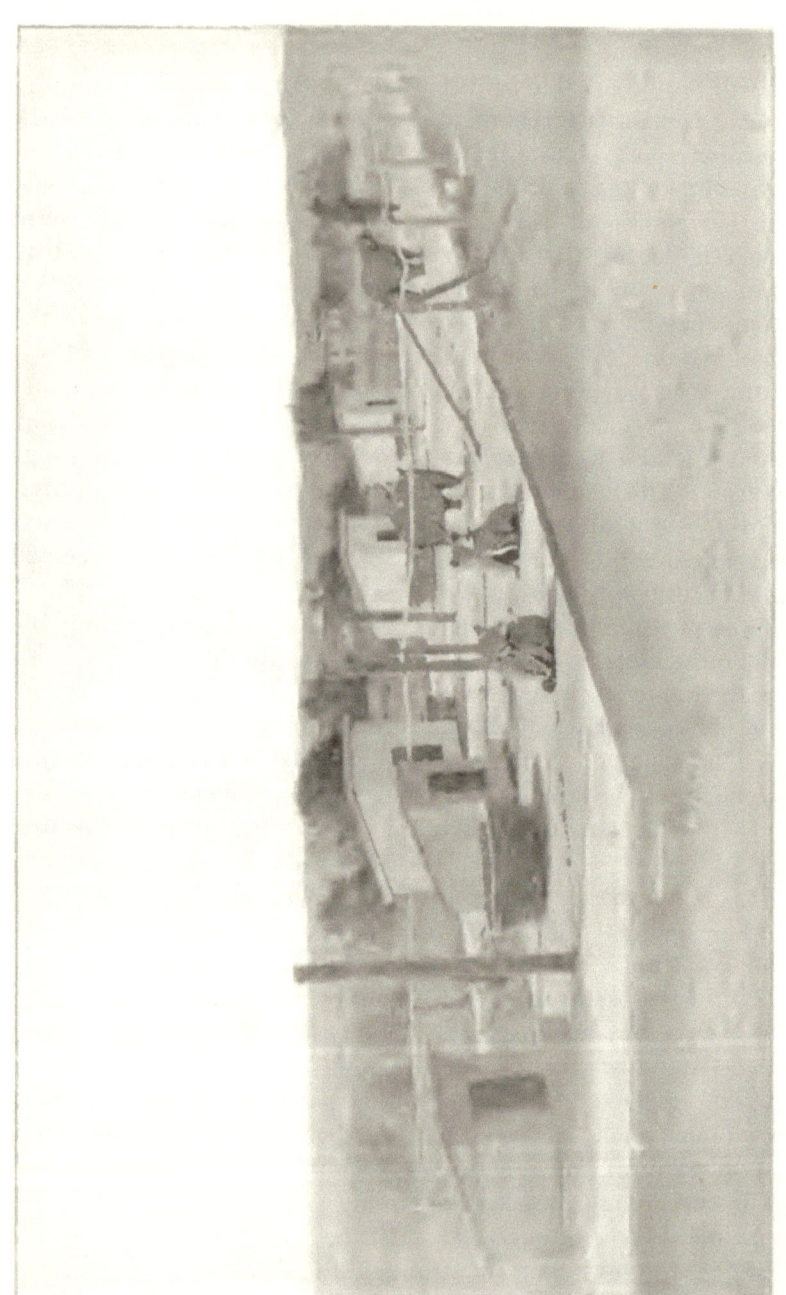

Bear at Hotel Roberval.

Having read your pleasing article in the Christmas number of *Fishing and Shooting*, I am tempted to write you, with the hope that you may have, or know where I may get, a photo of a point on the Ashuapmouchouan River called the Petite Chute of Portage à l'Ours. The point, 'View of River Mistassini,' used in the article, suggests strongly the Grande Chute, where three amateurs camped for nearly a week, and where I found more 'cussed vexation' crowded into a few days' experience than it had been ever my lot to meet with. On the train to Roberval we fell in with a young man ripe with Muskoka lore and legends, and in an untoward moment made him one of the party, trusting his superior skill in the gentle craft would prove a valuable help in our designs against the much 'Murrayed' ouananiche. We knew comparatively little about Walton's wiles, but were willing to learn. In a single day, our 'past grand knight of the rod' had succeeded in losing, in a pool, an excellent Conroy rod which we never recovered — his own property; managed to break my companion's rod; and when, towards evening, I had kindly loaned him mine, he hooked a fish and broke my only tip, having lost the other in a scramble over the rocks and amidst the undergrowth, whence I reached camp scratched, bruised, wet and disgusted with Canadian cross country, and firmly convinced that if the Montagnais aborigines made a circuit of three miles to reach a point of one mile — crow-flying distance—they had good reasons for it, amply sufficient, in fact, to overcome even Indian laziness. This little episode gave me a clearer and sorer idea of primitive woodcraft than the perusal of Cooper's fiction had ever furnished. Since that outing I have never read an account of Lac St. Jean without a feeling that if the writer should ever meet the shade of Ananias in the next world, he would be recognized at sight. My original companion proved a veritable Jonah, fishing the whole time; he never caught a whitefish, doré, or anything having a semblance of scales and fins. I have been often prompted to write up our trip, with the fond hope of deterring other misguided amateurs from dreaming of ouananiche; but knowing how sorely the compatriots of Patrice Clary and his Canadian fellow-guides need American dollars, I have restrained the itch of giving cold facts to ambitious tyros of the reel. I am yet possessed of the wish to try my luck again, and, I trust, under more favorable auspices. However, the bit of scenery which I mentioned in the first part of this letter has remained a bright spot in a dark setting. Perhaps you know its location and caught it with your camera. With the mosquitoes brushed away, it was the pleasantest ground we struck in our foolish expedition to find a jumping-off place in the North Pole direction. Trusting you may be able to comply with this (I hope not impertinent) request, I remain, etc."

This is an experience, indeed an especially amusing one, and rather out of the ordinary. The story of "cussed" fishing luck is exactly in line with what has been stated in the beginning of this chapter, and one that but few fishermen would so candidly relate. However, I can add that the writer did carry out his "wish to try my luck again," and the trip proved to be so thoroughly satisfactory, that he has often repeated the trial since.

Before concluding the chapter, and the work as well, some space properly should be devoted to—(the defence of, I was about to write in error)—the rarely excelled fighting powers of the ouananiche. Through the medium of occasional articles appearing in publications on fishing, a few letters received, and a very few complaints that I have heard personally, I find that an extremely small percentage of seekers after the Lake St. John fish raise the cry that its gameness is greatly overrated. I have referred to this subject several times in preceding chapters, but a final word cannot prove to be amiss.

I fear that these unbelievers must be classed as a variety of the "doubting Thomas" family, since they raise their voice or pen in opposition to the consensus of opinion as expressed by the most noted anglers in the country. All have hooked and brought to net, and at varying times during the season, ouananiche that were logy and faint-hearted. Such also has been the experience of those fortunate anglers who have met and conquered the salmon, bass and trout. They do not condemn them, however, for their inactivity at that particular time, since they know that history has credited them with battling powers which they are honestly entitled to. These same noted fishermen have made the history of the ouananiche as well, and the facts set forth would require more than the present very small minority vote to change them.

Any number of quotations from well-known fishing authorities could be given, but this is not at all necessary, since, as is well known, they all agree perfectly in regard to the fighting and lasting powers of the "little salmon." It is to be admitted that one cannot, as an enthusiast, write on a favorite subject without the recollection of past sport, and the imagination as well adding a little high coloring. Nature at times presents most gorgeous sunset hues and tints, colors, which if we were to describe or reproduce, would be classed as highly exaggerated. Why not, therefore, if Nature's occasional high colorings are natural and true, should not the occasional high-colored claims for the ouananiche be equally so?

In conclusion, I wish to state that the experiences given, the stories of the varying sport had, and the numbers of fish taken in catches mentioned, are not in the least out of the ordinary in any particular. The large number of sportsmen who have made not one alone, but a number of visits to and about Lake St. John, will almost universally give witness to this effect. Moreover, the fact must not be overlooked that the same possibilities for sport and success in fishing are still extant as in the past, and that thousands of square miles of virgin wilderness yet await the sportsman discoverer. Be governed by the when, where and how as set forth herein; then eliminate the attempt to accomplish all in a few days, or the inability to meet occasional disappointment, and but one result can follow—satisfaction and success heretofore unknown. You will feel amply repaid by seeing the wonderful beauties of the trip alone, but add to this the satisfaction of perfect sport secured, and you will return believing that the most satisfactory location for sportsmen to visit at the present day is Lake St. John and its surrounding wilderness.